THE QUEEN OF SHEBA

AND MY COUSIN THE

COLONEL

BY

THOMAS BAILEY ALDRICH

THE QUEEN OF SHEBA

I

MARY

In the month of June, 1872, Mr. Edward Lynde, the assistant cashier and bookkeeper of the Nautilus Bank at Rivermouth, found himself in a position to execute a plan which he had long meditated in secret.

A statement like this at the present time, when integrity in a place of trust has become almost an anomaly, immediately suggests a defalcation; but Mr. Lynde's plan involved nothing more criminal than a horseback excursion through the northern part of the State of New Hampshire. A leave of absence of three weeks, which had been accorded him in recognition of several years' conscientious service, offered young Lynde the opportunity he had desired. These three weeks, as already hinted, fell in the month of June, when Nature in New Hampshire is in her most ravishing toilet; she has put away her winter ermine, which sometimes serves her quite into spring; she has thrown a green mantle over her brown shoulders, and is not above the coquetry of wearing a great variety of wild flowers on her bosom. With her sassafras and her sweet-brier she is in her best mood, as a woman in a fresh and becoming costume is apt to be, and almost any one might mistake her laugh for the music of falling water, and the agreeable rustle of her garments for the wind blowing through the pine forests.

As Edward Lynde rode out of Rivermouth one morning, an hour or two before anybody worth mention was moving, he was very well contented with this world, though he had his grievances, too, if he had chosen to think of them.

Masses of dark cloud still crowded the zenith, but along the eastern horizon, against the increasing blue, lay a city of golden spires and mosques and minarets—an Oriental city, indeed, such as is inhabited by poets and dreamers and other speculative persons fond of investing their small capital in such unreal estate. Young Lynde, in spite of his prosaic profession of bookkeeper, had an opulent though as yet unworked vein of romance running through his composition, and he said to himself as he gave a slight twitch to the reins, "I'll put up there to-night at the sign of the Golden Fleece, or may be I'll quarter myself on one of those rich old merchants who used to do business with the bank in the colonial days." Before he had finished speaking the city was destroyed by a general conflagration; the round red sun rose slowly above the pearl-gray ruins, and it was morning.

In his three years' residence at Rivermouth, Edward Lynde had never chanced to see the town at so early an hour. The cobble-paved street through which he was riding was a commercial street; but now the shops had their wooden eyelids shut tight, and were snoozing away as comfortably and innocently as if they were not at all alive to a sharp stroke of business in their wakeful hours. There was a charm to Lynde in this novel phase of a thoroughfare so familiar to him, and then the morning was perfect. The street ran parallel with the river, the glittering harebell-blue of which could be seen across a vacant lot here and there, or now and then at the end of a narrow lane running up from the wharves. The atmosphere had that indescribable sparkle and bloom which last only an hour or so after daybreak, and was charged with fine sea-flavors and the delicate breath of dewy meadow-land. Everything appeared to exhale a fragrance; even the weather-beaten sign of "J. Tibbets & Son, West India Goods & Groceries," it seemed to Lynde, emitted an elusive spicy odor.

Edward Lynde soon passed beyond the limits of the town, and was ascending a steep hill, on the crest of which he proposed to take a farewell survey of the picturesque port throwing off its gauzy counterpane of sea-fog. The wind blew blithely on this hilltop; it filled his lungs and exhilarated him like champagne; he set spur to the gaunt, bony mare, and, with a flourish of his hand to the peaked roof of the Nautilus Bank, dashed off at a speed of not less than four miles an hour—for it was anything but an Arabian courser which Lynde had hired of honest Deacon Twombly. She was not a handsome animal either— yellow in tint and of the texture of an ancestral hair-trunk, with a plebeian head, and mysterious developments of muscle on the hind legs. She was not a horse for fancy riding; but she had her good points—she had a great many points of one kind and another—among which was her perfect adaptability to rough country roads and the sort of work now required of her.

"Mary ain't what you'd call a racer," Deacon Twombly had remarked while the negotiations were pending; "I don't say she is, but she's easy on the back."

This statement was speedily verified. At the end of two miles Mary stopped short and began backing, deliberately and systematically, as if to slow music in a circus. Recovering from the surprise of the halt, which had taken him wholly unawares, Lynde gathered the slackened reins firmly in his hand and pressed his spurs to the mare's flanks, with no other effect than slightly to accelerate the backward movement.

Perhaps nothing gives you so acute a sense of helplessness as to have a horse back with you, under the saddle or between shafts. The reins lie limp in your hands, as if detached from the animal; it is impossible to check him or force him forward; to turn him around is to confess yourself conquered; to descend and take him by the head is an act of pusillanimity. Of course there is only one thing to be done; but if you know what that is you possess a singular advantage over your fellow-creatures.

Finding spur and whip of no avail, Lynde tried the effect of moral suasion: he stroked Mary on the neck, and addressed her in terms that would have melted the heart of almost any other Mary; but she continued to back, slowly and with a certain grace that could have come only of confirmed habit. Now Lynde had no desire to return to Rivermouth, above all to back into it in that mortifying fashion and make himself a spectacle for the townsfolk; but if this thing went on forty or fifty minutes longer, that would be the result.

"If I cannot stop her," he reflected, "I'll desert the brute just before we get to the toll-gate. I can't think what possessed Twombly to let me have such a ridiculous animal!"

Mary showed no sign that she was conscious of anything unconventional or unlooked for in her conduct.

"Mary, my dear," said Lynde at last, with dangerous calmness, "you would be all right, or, at least, your proceeding would not be quite so flagrant a breach of promise, if you were only aimed in the opposite direction."

With this he gave a vigorous jerk at the left-hand rein, which caused the mare to wheel about and face Rivermouth. She hesitated an instant, and then resumed backing.

"Now, Mary," said the young man dryly, "I will let you have your head, so to speak, as long as you go the way I want you to."

This manoeuvre on the side of Lynde proved that he possessed qualities which, if skilfully developed, would have assured him success in the higher regions of domestic diplomacy. The ability to secure your own way and impress others with the idea that they are having THEIR own way is rare among men; among women it is as common as eyebrows.

"I wonder how long she will keep this up," mused Lynde, fixing his eye speculatively on Mary's pull-back ears. "If it is to be a permanent arrangement I shall have to reverse the saddle. Certainly, the creature is a lusus naturae— her head is on the wrong end! Easy on the back," he added, with a hollow laugh, recalling Deacon Twombly's recommendation. "I should say she was! I never saw an easier."

Presently Mary ceased her retrograde movement, righted herself of her own accord, and trotted off with as much submissiveness as could be demanded of her. Lynde subsequently learned that this propensity to back was an unaccountable whim which seized Mary at odd intervals and lasted from five to fifteen minutes. The peculiarity once understood not only ceased to be an annoyance to him, but became an agreeable break in the ride. Whenever her mood approached, he turned the mare round and let her back to her soul's content. He also ascertained that the maximum of Mary's speed was five miles an hour.

"I didn't want a fast horse, anyway," said Lynde philosophically. "As I am not going anywhere in particular, I need be in no hurry to get there."

The most delightful feature of Lynde's plan was that it was not a plan. He had simply ridden off into the rosy June weather, with no settled destination, no care for to-morrow, and as independent as a bird of the tourist's ordinary requirements. At the crupper of his saddle—an old cavalry saddle that had seen service in long-forgotten training-days—was attached a cylindrical valise of cowhide, containing a change of linen, a few toilet articles, a vulcanized cloth cape for rainy days, and the first volume of The Earthly Paradise. The two warlike holsters in front (in which Colonel Eliphalet Bangs used to carry a brace of flintlock pistols now reposing in the Historical Museum at Rivermouth) became the receptacle respectively of a slender flask of brandy and a Bologna sausage; for young Lynde had determined to sell his life dearly if by any chance of travel he came to close quarters with famine.

A broad-brimmed Panama hat, a suit of navy-blue flannel, and a pair of riding-boots completed his equipment. A field-glass in a leather case was swung by a strap over his shoulder, and in the breast pocket of his blouse he carried a small compass to guide him on his journey due north.

The young man's costume went very well with his frank, refined face, and twenty-three years. A dead-gold mustache, pointed at the ends and sweeping at a level right and left, like a swallow's wings, gave him something of a military air; there was a martial directness, too, in the glance of his clear gray eyes, undimmed as yet with looking too long on the world. There could not have been a better figure for the saddle than Lynde's—slightly above the average height, straight as a poplar, and neither too spare nor too heavy. Now and then, as he passed a farm-house, a young girl hanging out clothes in the front yard—for it was on a Monday—would pause with a shapeless snowdrift in her hand to gaze curiously at the apparition of a gallant young horseman riding by. It often happened that when he had passed, she would slyly steal to the red gate in the lichen-covered stone wall, and follow him with her palm-shaded eyes down the lonely road; and it as frequently happened that he would glance back over his shoulder at the nut-brown maid, whose closely clinging, scant drapery gave her a sculpturesque grace to which her unconsciousness of it was a charm the more.

These flashes of subtile recognition between youth and youth—these sudden mute greetings and farewells—reached almost the dimension of incidents in that first day's eventless ride. Once Lynde halted at the porch of a hip-roofed, unpainted house with green paper shades at the windows, and asked for a cup of milk, which was brought him by the nut-brown maid, who never took her flattering innocent eyes off the young man's face while he drank—sipping him as he sipped the milk; and young Lynde rode away feeling as if something had really happened.

More than once that morning he drew up by the roadside to listen to some lyrical robin on an apple-bough, or to make friends with the black-belted Durham cows and the cream-colored Alderneys, who came solemnly to the pasture wall and stared at him with big, good-natured faces. A row of them, with their lazy eyes and pink tongues and moist india-rubber noses, was as good as a play.

At noon that day our adventureless adventurer had reached Bayley's Four-Corners, where he found provender for himself and Mary at what had formerly been a tavern, in the naive stage-coach epoch. It was the sole house in the neighborhood, and was occupied by the ex-landlord, one Tobias Sewell, who had turned farmer. On finishing his cigar after dinner, Lynde put the saddle on Mary, and started forward again. It is hardly correct to say forward, for Mary took it into her head to back out of Bayley's Four-Corners, a feat which she performed to the unspeakable amusement of Mr. Sewell and a quaint old gentleman, named Jaffrey, who boarded in the house.

"I guess that must be a suck-cuss hoss," remarked Mr. Sewell, resting his loosely jointed figure against the rail fence as he watched his departing guest.

Mary backed to the ridge of the hill up which the turnpike stretched from the ancient tavern, then recovered herself and went on.

"I never saw such an out-and-out wilful old girl as you are, Mary!" ejaculated Lynde, scarlet with mortification. "I begin to admire you."

Perhaps the covert reproach touched some finer chord of Mary's nature, or perhaps Mary had done her day's allowance of backing; whatever the case was, she indulged no further caprice that afternoon beyond shying vigorously at a heavily loaded tin-pedler's wagon, a proceeding which may be palliated by the statement of the fact that many of Mary's earlier years were passed in connection with a similar establishment.

The afterglow of sunset had faded out behind the serrated line of hills, and black shadows were assembling, like conspirators, in the orchards and under the spreading elms by the roadside, when Edward Lynde came in sight of a large manufacturing town, which presented a sufficiently bizarre appearance at that hour.

Grouped together in a valley were five or six high, irregular buildings, illuminated from basement to roof, each with a monstrous chimney from which issued a fan of party-colored flame. On one long low structure, with a double row of windows gleaming like the port-holes of a man-of-war at night, was a squat round tower that now and then threw open a vast valve at the top, and belched forth a volume of amber smoke, which curled upward to a dizzy height and spread itself out against the sky. Lying in the weird light of these chimneys, with here and there a gable or a spire suddenly outlined in vivid purple, the huddled town beneath seemed like an outpost of the infernal regions. Lynde, however, resolved to spend the night there instead of riding on farther and trusting for shelter to some farm-house or barn. Ten or twelve hours in the saddle had given him a keen appetite for rest.

Presently the roar of flues and furnaces, and the resonant din of mighty hammers beating against plates of iron, fell upon his ear; a few minutes later he rode into the town, not knowing and not caring in the least what town it was.

All this had quite the flavor of foreign travel to Lynde, who began pondering on which hotel he should bestow his patronage—a question that sometimes perplexes the tourist on arriving at a strange city. In Lynde's case the matter was considerably simplified by the circumstance that there was but a single aristocratic hotel in the place. He extracted this information from a small boy, begrimed with iron-dust, and looking as if he had just been cast at a neighboring foundry, who kindly acted as cicerone, and conducted the tired wayfarer to the doorstep of The Spread Eagle, under one of whose wings—to be at once figurative and literal—he was glad to nestle for the night.

II

IN WHICH THERE IS A FAMILY JAR

While Lynde is enjoying the refreshing sleep that easily overtook him after supper, we will reveal to the reader so much of the young man's private history as may be necessary to the narrative. In order to do this, the author, like Deacon Twombly's mare, feels it indispensable to back a little.

One morning, about three years previous to the day when Edward Lynde set forth on his aimless pilgrimage, Mr. Jenness Bowlsby, the president of the Nautilus Bank at Rivermouth, received the following letter from his wife's nephew, Mr. John Flemming, a young merchant in New York—

NEW YORK, May 28, 1869.

MY DEAR UNCLE: In the course of a few days a friend of mine, Mr. Edward Lynde of this city, will call upon you and hand you a note of introduction from myself. I write this to secure for him in advance the liking and interest which I am persuaded you will not be able to withhold on closer acquaintance. I have been intimate with Edward Lynde for twelve years or more, first at the boarding-school at Flatbush, and afterwards at college. Though several years my junior, he was in the same classes with me, and, if the truth must be told, generally carried off all the honors. He is not only the most accomplished young fellow I know, but a fellow of inexhaustible modesty and amiability, and I think it was singularly malicious of destiny to pick him out as a victim, when there are so many worthless young men (the name of John Flemming will instantly occur to you) who deserve nothing better than rough treatment. You see, I am taking point-blank aim at your sympathy.

When Lynde was seven or eight years old he had the misfortune to lose his mother; his father was already dead. The child's nearest relative was an uncle, David Lynde, a rich merchant of New York, a bachelor, and a character. Old Lynde—I call him old Lynde not out of disrespect, but to distinguish him from young Lynde—was at that period in his sixtieth year, a gentleman of unsullied commercial reputation, and of regular if somewhat peculiar habits. He was at his counting-room precisely at eight in the morning, and was the last to leave in the evening, working as many hours each day as he had done in those first years when he entered as office-boy into the employment of Briggs & Livingstone—the firm at the time of which I am now writing was Lynde, Livingstone & Co. Mr. David Lynde lived in a set of chambers up town, and dined at his club, where he usually passed the evenings at chess with some brother antediluvian. A visit to the theatre, when some old English comedy or some new English ballet happened to be on the boards, was the periphery of his dissipation. What is called society saw nothing of him. He was a rough, breezy, thickset old gentleman, betrothed from his birth to apoplexy, enjoying life in his own secluded manner, and insisting on having everybody about him happy. He would strangle an old friend rather than not have him happy. A characteristic story is told of a quarrel he had with a chum of thirty or forty years' standing, Ripley Sturdevant Sen. Sturdevant came to grief in the financial panic of 1857. Lynde held a mortgage on Sturdevant's house, and insisted on cancelling it. Sturdevant refused to accept the sacrifice. They both were fiery old gentlemen, arcades ambo. High words ensued. What happened never definitely transpired; but Sturdevant was found lying across the office lounge, with a slight bruise over one eyebrow and the torn mortgage thrust into his shirt-bosom. It was conjectured that Lynde had actually knocked him down and forced the cancelled mortgage upon him!

In short, David Lynde was warm-hearted and generous to the verge of violence, but a man in every way unfitted by temperament, experience, and mode of life to undertake the guardianship of a child. To have an infant dropped into his arms was as excellent an imitation of a calamity as could well happen to him. I am told that no one could have been more sensible of this than David Lynde himself, and that there was something extremely touching in the alacrity and cheerfulness with which he assumed the novel responsibility.

Immediately after the funeral—Mrs. Lynde had resided in Philadelphia—the uncle brought the boy to New York. It was impossible to make a permanent home for young Lynde in bachelor chambers, or to dine him at the club. After a week of inconvenience and wretchedness, complicated by the sinister suspicions of his landlady, David Lynde concluded to send the orphan to boarding-school.

It was at Flatbush, Long Island, that I made the acquaintance of the forlorn little fellow. His cot was next to mine in the dormitory; we became close friends. We passed our examinations, left Flatbush at the same time, and entered college together. In the meanwhile the boy's relations with his guardian were limited to a weekly exchange of letters, those of the uncle invariably beginning with "Yours of Saturday duly at hand," and ending with "Enclosed please find." In respect to pocket-money young Lynde was a prince. My friend spent the long vacations with me at Newburgh, running down to New York occasionally to pass a day or so with the uncle. In these visits their intimacy ripened. Old Lynde was now become very proud of his bright young charge, giving him astonishing dinners at Delmonico's, taking him to Wallack's, and introducing him to the old fossils at the club as "my boy Ned."

It was at the beginning of Lynde's last term at college that his uncle retired from business, bought a house in Madison Avenue, and turned it into a sort of palace with frescoes and upholstery. There was a library for my boy Ned, a smoking-room in cherry-wood, a billiard-room in black walnut, a dining-room in oak and crimson—in brief, the beau-ideal of a den for a couple of bachelors. By Jove! it was like a club-house—the only model for a home of which poor old Lynde had any conception. Six months before Ned was graduated, the establishment was in systematic running order under the supervision of the pearl of housekeepers. Here David Lynde proposed to spend the rest of his days with his nephew, who might, for form's sake, adopt some genteel profession; if not, well and good, the boy would have money.

Now just as Ned was carrying off the first prizes in Greek and mathematics, and dreaming of the pleasant life he was to lead with his amiable old benefactor, what does that amiable old benefactor go and do but marry the housekeeper!

David Lynde knew very little of women: he had not spoken to above a dozen in his whole life; did not like them, in fact; had a mild sort of contempt for them, as persons devoid of business ability. It was in the course of nature that the first woman who thought it worth her while should twist him around her finger like a remnant of ribbon. When Ned came out of college he found himself in the arms of an unlooked-for aunt who naturally hated him at sight.

I have not the time or space, my dear uncle, to give you even a catalogue of the miseries that followed on the heels of this deplorable marriage; besides, you can imagine them. Old Lynde, loving both his wife and his nephew, was by turns violent and feeble; the wife cool, cunning, and insidious—a Vivien of forty leading Merlin by the beard. I am not prepared to contend that the nephew was always in the right, but I know he always got the worst of it, which amounts to about the same thing. At the end of eight or ten months he saw that the position was untenable, packed his trunk one night, and quitted the MENAGE—the menagerie, as he calls it.

This was three weeks ago. Having a small property of his own, some fifteen hundred dollars a year, I believe, Lynde at first thought to go abroad. It was always his dream to go abroad. But I persuaded him out of that, seeing how perilous it would be for a young fellow of his inexperience and impressible disposition to go rambling alone over the Continent. Paris was his idea. Paris would not make a mouthful of him. I have talked him out of that, I repeat, and have succeeded in convincing him that the wisest course for him to pursue is to go to some pleasant town or village within hailing distance of one of our larger cities, and spend the summer quietly. I even suggested he should make the personal acquaintance of some light employment, to help him forget the gorgeous castle of cards which has just tumbled down about his ears. In six words, I have sent him to Rivermouth.

Now, my dear uncle, I have wasted eight pages of paper and probably a hundred dollars' worth of your time, if you do not see that I am begging you to find a position for Lynde in the Nautilus Bank. After a little practice he would make a skilful accountant, and the question of salary is, as you see, of secondary importance. Manage to retain him at Rivermouth if you possibly can. David Lynde has the strongest affection for the lad, and if Vivien, whose name is Elizabeth, is not careful how she drags Merlin around by the beard, he will reassert himself in some unexpected manner. If he were to serve her as he is supposed to have served old Sturdevant, his conduct would be charitably criticised. If he lives a year he will be in a frame of mind to leave the bulk of his fortune to Ned. THEY have not quarrelled, you understand; on the contrary, Mr. Lynde was anxious to settle an allowance of five thousand a year on Ned, but Ned would not accept it. "I want uncle David's love," says Ned, "and I have it; the devil take his money."

Here you have all the points. I could not state them more succinctly and do justice to each of the parties interested. The most unfortunate party, I take it, is David Lynde. I am not sure, after all, that young Lynde is so much to be pitied. Perhaps that club-house would not have worked well for him if it had worked differently. At any rate he now has his own way to make, and I commend him to your kindness, if I have not exhausted it.

Your affectionate nephew, J. FLEMMING.

Five or six days after this letter reached Mr. Bowlsby, Mr. Edward Lynde presented himself in the directors' room of the Nautilus Bank. The young man's bearing confirmed the favorable impression which Mr. Bowlsby had derived from his nephew's letter, and though there was really no vacancy in the bank at the moment, Mr. Bowlsby lent himself to the illusion that he required a private secretary. A few weeks later a vacancy occurred unexpectedly, that of paying-teller—a position in which Lynde acquitted himself with so much quickness and accuracy, that when Mr. Trefethen, the assistant cashier, died in the December following, Lynde was promoted to his desk.

The unruffled existence into which Edward Lynde had drifted was almost the reverse of the career he had mapped out for himself, and it was a matter of mild astonishment to him at intervals that he was not discontented. He thought Rivermouth one of the most charming old spots he had ever seen or heard of, and the people the most hospitable. The story of his little family jar, taking deeper colors and richer ornamentation as it passed from hand to hand, made him at once a social success. Mr. Goldstone, one of the leading directors of the bank, invited Lynde to dinner—few persons were ever overburdened with invitations to dine at the Goldstones'—and the door of many a refined home turned willingly on its hinges for the young man. At the evening parties, that winter, Edward Lynde was considered almost as good a card as a naval officer. Miss Mildred Bowlsby, then the reigning belle, was ready to flirt with him to the brink of the Episcopal marriage service, and beyond; but the phenomenal honeymoon which had recently quartered in Lynde's family left him indisposed to take any lunar observations on his own account.

With his salary as cashier, Lynde's income was Vanderbiltish for a young man in Rivermouth. Unlike his great contemporary, he did not let it accumulate. Once a month he wrote a dutiful letter to his uncle David, who never failed to answer by telegraph, "Yours received. God bless you, Edward." This whimsical fashion of reply puzzled young Lynde quite as much as it diverted him until he learned (through his friend, John Flemming) that his aunt Vivien had extorted from the old gentleman a solemn promise not to write to his nephew.

Lynde's duties at the bank left him free every afternoon at four o'clock; his work and his leisure were equally pleasant. In summer he kept a sail-boat on the river, and in winter he had the range of a rich collection of books connected with an antiquated public reading-room. Thus very happily, if very quietly, and almost imperceptibly the months rolled round to that period when the Nautilus Bank gave Edward Lynde a three weeks' vacation, and he set forth, as we have seen, on Deacon Twombly's mare, in search of the picturesque and the peculiar, if they were to be found in the northern part of New Hampshire.

III

IN WHICH MARY TAKES A NEW DEPARTURE

It was still dark enough the next morning to allow the great chimneys to show off their colored fires effectively, when Lynde passed through the dingy main street of K—-and struck into a road which led to the hill country. A short distance beyond the town, while he was turning in the saddle to observe the singular effect of the lurid light upon the landscape, a freight-train shot obliquely across the road within five rods of his horse's head, the engine flinging great flakes of fiery spume from its nostrils, and shrieking like a maniac as it plunged into a tunnel through a spur of the hills. Mary went sideways, like a crab, for the next three quarters of a mile.

To most young men the expedition which Edward Lynde had undertaken would have seemed unattractive and monotonous to the last degree; but Lynde's somewhat sedentary habits had made him familiar with his own company. When one is young and well read and amiable, there is really no better company than one's self—as a steady thing. We are in a desperate strait indeed if we chance at any age to tire of this invisible but ever-present comrade; for he is not to be thrown over during life. Before now, men have become so weary of him, so bored by him, that they have attempted to escape, by suicide; but it is a question if death itself altogether rids us of him.

In no minute of the twenty-four hours since Lynde left Rivermouth had he felt the want of other companionship. Mary, with her peculiarities, the roadside sights and sounds, the chubby children with shining morning face, on the way to school, the woodland solitudes, the farmers at work in the fields, the blue jays and the robins in the orchards, the blonde and brown girls at the cottage doors, his own buoyant, unreproachful thoughts—what need had he of company? If anything could have added to his enjoyment it would have been the possibility of being waylaid by bandits, or set upon in some desolate pass by wild animals. But, alas, the nearest approximation to a bandit that fell in his way was some shabby, spiritless tramp who passed by on the further side without lifting an eyelid; and as for savage animals, he saw nothing more savage than a monkish chipmunk here and there, who disappeared into his stonewall convent the instant he laid eyes on Lynde.

Riding along those lonely New England roads, he was more secure than if he had been lounging in the thronged avenues of a great city. Certainly he had dropped on an age and into a region sterile of adventure. He felt this, but not so sensitively as to let it detract from the serene pleasure he found in it all. From the happy glow of his mind every outward object took a rosy light; even a rustic funeral, which he came upon at a cross-road that fore-noon, softened itself into something not unpicturesque.

For three days after quitting K—-Lynde pushed steadily forward. The first two nights he secured lodgings at a farm-house; on the third night he was regarded as a suspicious character, and obtained reluctant permission to stow himself in a hay-loft, where he was so happy at roughing it and being uncomfortable that he could scarcely close an eye. The amateur outcast lay dreamily watching the silver spears of moonlight thrust through the roof of the barn, and extracting such satisfaction from his cheerless surroundings as would have astonished a professional tramp. "Poverty and hardship are merely ideas after all," said Lynde to himself softly, as he drifted off in a doze. Ah, Master Lynde, playing at poverty and hardship is one thing; but if the reality is merely an idea, it is one of the very worst ideas in the world.

The young man awoke before sunrise the next morning, and started onward without attempting to negotiate for breakfast with his surly host. He had faith that some sunburnt young woman, with bowl of brown-bread and milk, would turn up farther on; if she did not, and no tavern presented itself, there were the sausage and the flask of eau-de-vie still untouched in the holsters.

The mountain air had not wholly agreed with Mary, who at this stage of the journey inaugurated a series of abnormal coughs, each one of which went near to flinging Lynde out of the saddle.

"Mary," he said, after a particularly narrow escape, "there are few fine accomplishments you haven't got except a spavin. Perhaps you've got that, concealed somewhere about your person."

He said this in a tone of airy badinage which Mary seemed to appreciate; but he gravely wondered what he could do with her, and how he should replace her, if she fell seriously ill.

For the last two days farm-houses and cultivated fields had been growing rarer and rarer, and the road rougher and wilder. At times it made a sudden detour, to avoid the outcropping of a monster stratum of granite, and in places became so narrow that the rank huckleberry-bushes swept the mare's flanks. Lynde found it advisable on the morning in question to pick his way carefully. A range of arid hills rose darkly before him, stretching east and west further than his eye could follow—rugged, forlorn hills covered with a thick prickly undergrowth, and sentinelled by phantom-like pines. There were gloomy, rocky gorges on each hand, and high-hanging crags, and where the vapor was drawn aside like a veil, in one place, he saw two or three peaks with what appeared to be patches of snow on them. Perhaps they were merely patches of bleached rock.

Long afterwards, when Edward Lynde was passing through the valley of the Arve, on the way from Geneva to Chamouni, he recollected this bit of Switzerland in America, and it brought an odd, perplexed smile to his lips.

The thousand ghostly shapes of mist which had thronged the heights, shutting in the prospect on every side, had now vanished, discovering as wild and melancholy a spot as a romantic heart could desire. There was something sinister and ironical even in the sunshine that lighted up these bleak hills. The silver waters of a spring—whose source was hidden somewhere high up among the mossy boulders—dripping silently from ledge to ledge, had the pathos of tears. The deathly stillness was broken only by the dismal caw of a crow taking abrupt flight from a blasted pine. Here and there a birch with its white satin skin glimmered spectrally among the sombre foliage.

The inarticulate sadness of the place brought a momentary feeling of depression to Lynde, who was not usually given to moods except of the lighter sort. He touched Mary sharply with the spurs and cantered up the steep.

He had nearly gained the summit of the hill when he felt the saddle slipping; the girth had unbuckled or broken. As he dismounted, the saddle came off with him, his foot still in the stirrup. The mare shied, and the rein slipped from his fingers; he clutched at it, but Mary gave a vicious toss of the head, wheeled about, and began trotting down the declivity. Her trot at once broke into a gallop, and the gallop into a full run—a full run for Mary. At the foot of the hill she stumbled, fell, rolled over, gathered herself up, and started off again at increased speed. The road was perfectly straight for a mile or two. The horse was already a small yellow patch in the distance. She was evidently on her way back to Rivermouth! Lynde watched her until she was nothing but a speck against the gray road, then he turned and cast a rueful glance on the saddle, which suddenly took to itself a satirical aspect, as it lay sprawling on the ground at his feet.

He had been wanting something to happen, and something had happened. He was unhorsed and alone in the heart of the hill country—alone in a strange and, it seemed to Lynde as he looked about him, uninhabited region.

IV

THE ODD ADVENTURE WHICH BEFELL YOUNG LYNDE IN THE HILL COUNTRY

It had all happened so suddenly that one or two minutes passed before Edward Lynde took in the full enormity of Mary's desertion. A dim smile was still hovering about his lips when the yellow speck that was Mary faded into the gray distance; then his countenance fell. There was no sign of mortal habitation visible from the hillside where he stood; the farm at which he had spent the night was five miles away; his stiff riding-boots were ill-adapted to pedestrianism. The idea of lugging that heavy saddle five miles over a mountain road caused him to knit his brows and look very serious indeed. As he gave the saddle an impatient kick, his eyes rested on the Bologna sausage, one end of which protruded from the holster; then there came over him a poignant recollection of his Lenten supper of the night before and his no breakfast at all of that morning. He seated himself on the saddle, unwrapped the sausage, and proceeded to cut from it two or three thin slices.

"It might have been much worse," he reflected, as he picked off with his penknife the bits of silver foil which adhered to the skin of the sausage; "if Mary had decamped with the commissary stores, that would have been awkward." Lynde devoured the small pieces of pressed meat with an appetite born of his long fast and the bracing upland air.

"Talk about pate de foie gras!" he exclaimed, with a sweep of his arm, as if he were disdainfully waving back a menial bearing a tray of Strasbourg pates; "if I live to return to Rivermouth I will have Bologna sausage three times a day for the rest of my life."

A cup of the ice-cold water which bubbled up from a boss of cresses by the roadside completed his Spartan breakfast. His next step was to examine his surroundings. "From the top of this hill," said Lynde, "I shall probably be able to see where I am, if that will be any comfort to me."

It was only fifty or sixty rods to the crown of the hill, where the road, viewed from below, seemed abruptly to come to an end against the sky. On gaining the summit, Lynde gave an involuntary exclamation of surprise and delight. At his feet in the valley below, in a fertile plain walled in on all sides by the emerald slopes, lay the loveliest village that ever was seen. Though the road by which he had approached the eminence had been narrow and steep, here it widened and descended by gentle gradations into the valley, where it became the main street of the village—a congregation of two or possibly three hundred houses, mostly cottages with gambrel and lean-to roofs. At the left of the village, and about an eighth of a mile distant, was an imposing red brick building with wings and a pair of octagon towers. It stood in a forest of pines and maples, and appeared to be enclosed by a high wall of masonry. It was too pretentious for an almshouse, too elegant for a prison; it was as evidently not a school-house, and it could not be an arsenal. Lynde puzzled over it a moment, and then returned for his saddle, which he slung across his back, holding it by a stirrup-strap brought over either shoulder.

"If Mary has got a conscience," muttered Lynde, "it would prick her if she could see me now. I must be an affecting spectacle. In the village they won't know whether I am the upper or the lower half of a centaur. They won't know whether to rub me down and give me a measure of oats, or to ask me in to breakfast."

The saddle with its trappings probably weighed forty pounds, and Lynde was glad before he had accomplished a third of the way to the village to set down his burden and rest awhile. On each side of him now were cornfields, and sloping orchards peopled with those grotesque, human-like apple-trees which seem twisted and cramped by a pain possibly caught from their own acidulous fruit. The cultivated land terminated only where the village began. It was not so much a village as a garden—a garden crowded with flowers of that bright metallic tint which distinguishes the flora of northern climes. Through the centre of this Eden ran the wide main street, fringed with poplars and elms and chestnuts. No polluting brewery or smoky factory, with its hideous architecture, marred the idyllic beauty of the miniature town—for everything which is not a city is a town in New England. The population obviously consisted of well-to-do persons, with outlying stock-farms or cranberry meadows, and funds snugly invested in ships and railroads.

In out-of-the-way places like this is preserved the greater part of what we have left of the hard shrewd sense and the simpler manner of those homespun old worthies who planted the seed of the Republic. In our great cities we are cosmopolitans; but here we are Americans of the primitive type, or as nearly as may be. It was unimportant settlements like the one we are describing that sent their quota of stout hearts and flintlock muskets to the trenches on Bunker Hill. Here, too, the valorous spirit which had been slumbering on its arm for half a century started up at the first shot fired against Fort Sumter. Over the chimney-place of more than one cottage in such secluded villages hangs an infantry or a cavalry sword in its dinted sheath, looked at to-day by wife or mother with the tenderly proud smile that has mercifully taken the place of tears.

Beyond the town, on the hillside which Edward Lynde had just got within the focus of his field-glass, was the inevitable cemetery. On a grave here and there a tiny flag waved in the indolent June breeze. If Lynde had been standing by the head-stones, he could have read among the inscriptions such unlocal words as Malvern Hill, Andersonville, Ball's Bluff, and Gettysburg, and might have seen the withered Decoration Day wreaths which had been fresh the month before.

Lynde brought his glass to bear on the red brick edifice mentioned, and fell to pondering it again.

"I'll be hanged if I don't think it's a nunnery," he said. By and by he let his gaze wander back to the town, in which he detected an appearance of liveliness and bustle not usual in New England villages, large or small. The main street was dotted with groups of men and women; and isolated figures, to which perhaps the distance lent a kind of uncanny aspect, were to be seen hurrying hither and thither.

"It must be some local celebration," thought Lynde. "Rural oratory and all that sort of thing. That will be capital!"

He had returned the glass to its leather case, and was settling it well on his hip, when he saw a man approaching. It was a heavily built old gentleman in a suit of black alpaca, somewhat frayed and baggy at the knees, but still respectable. He carried his hat in his hand, fanning himself with it from time to time, as if overcome by heat and the fatigue of walking. A profusion of snow-white hair, parted in the middle, swept down on either side of a face remarkable—if it was remarkable for anything—for its benign and simple expression. There was a far-off, indescribable something about this person, as though he had existed long ago and once had a meaning, but was now become an obsolete word in the human dictionary. His wide placid brows and the double chin which asserted itself above his high neckcloth gave him a curious resemblance to portraits of Dr. Franklin.

"The country parson," said Lynde to himself. "Venerable and lovely old character. I'll speak to him."

The old gentleman, with his head slightly thrown back, had his eyes fixed intently on some object in the sky, and was on the point of passing Lynde without observing him, when the young man politely lifted his hat, and said, "I beg your pardon, sir, but will you be kind enough to tell me the name of the town yonder?"

The old gentleman slowly brought his eyes down from the sky, fixed them vacantly upon Lynde, and made no response. Presuming him to be deaf, Lynde repeated his question in a key adapted to the exigency. Without a change in his mild, benevolent expression, and in a voice whose modulations were singularly musical, the old gentleman exclaimed, "Go to the devil!" and passed on.

The rejoinder was so unexpected, the words themselves were so brusque, while the utterance was so gentle and melodious, that Lynde refused to credit his ears. Could he have heard aright? Before he recovered from his surprise the gentleman in black was far up the slope, his gaze again riveted on some remote point in the zenith.

"It wasn't the country parson after all," said Lynde, with a laugh; "it was the village toper. He's an early bird—I'll say that for him—to have secured his intoxicating worm at this hour of the morning."

Lynde picked up the saddle and resumed his march on the town in the happy valley. He had proceeded only a little way when he perceived another figure advancing towards him—a figure not less striking than that of the archaic gentleman, but quite different. This was a young girl, of perhaps seventeen, in a flowing dress of some soft white stuff, gathered at the waist by a broad red ribbon. She was without hat or shawl, and wore her hair, which was very long and very black, hanging loosely down her shoulders, in exaggeration of a style of coiffure that afterwards came into fashion. She was moving slowly and in the manner of a person not accustomed to walking. She was a lady— Lynde saw that at a glance—probably some city-bred bird of passage, resting for the summer in this vale of health. His youthful vanity took alarm as he reflected what a comical picture he must present with that old saddle on his back. He would have dumped it into the barberry-bushes if he could have done so unobserved; but it was now too late.

On perceiving Lynde, the girl arrested her steps a moment irresolutely, and then came directly towards him. As she drew nearer Lynde was conscious of being dazzled by a pair of heavily fringed black eyes, large and lustrous, set in an oval face of exquisite pallor. The girl held a dandelion in one hand, twirling it by the end of its long, snake-like stem as she approached. She was close upon him now; for an instant he caught the wind of the flower as it swiftly described a circle within an inch of his cheek. The girl paused in front of him, and drawing herself up to her full height said haughtily—

"I am the Queen of Sheba."

Then she glided by him with a quickened pace and a suddenly timid air. Lynde was longer recovering himself, this time. He stood rooted to the ground, stupidly watching the retreating gracious form of the girl, who half turned once and looked back at him. Then she vanished over the ridge of the hill, as the old gentleman had done. Was she following him? Was there any connection between those two? Perhaps he was the village clergyman. Could this be his daughter? What an unconventional costume for a young lady to promenade in—for she was a lady down to her finger-nails! And what an odd salutation!

"The Queen of Sheba!" he repeated wonderingly. "What could she mean by that? She took me for some country bumpkin, with this confounded saddle, and was laughing at me. I never saw a girl at once so—so audacious and modest, or so lovely. I didn't know there was anything on earth so lovely as that girl."

He had caught only an instantaneous glimpse of her face, but he had seen it with strange distinctness, as one sees an object by a flash of lightning; and he still saw it, as one seems still to see the object in the after-darkness. Every line of the features lived in his eyes, even an almost indistinguishable scar there was on the girl's right cheek near the temple. It was not a flaw, that faint scar; it seemed somehow to heighten her loveliness, as an accent over a word sometimes gives it one knows not what of piquancy.

"Evidently she lives in the town or in the neighborhood. Shall I meet her again, I wonder? I will stay here a week or a month if—What nonsense! I must have distinguished myself, staring at her like a gawk. When she said she was the

Queen of Sheba, I ought instantly to have replied—what in the deuce is it I ought to have replied? How can a man be witty with a ton of sole-leather pressing on his spine!"

Edward Lynde, with the girl and her mocking words in his mind, and busying himself with all the clever things he might have said and did not say, mechanically traversed the remaining distance to the village.

The street which had seemed thronged when he viewed it from the slope of the hill was deserted; at the farther end he saw two or three persons hurrying along, but there were no indications whatever of the festival he had conjectured. Indeed, the town presented the appearance of a place smitten by a pestilence. The blinds of the lower casements of all the houses were closed; he would have supposed them unoccupied if he had not caught sight of a face pressed against the glass of an upper window here and there. He thought it singular that these faces instantly withdrew when he looked up. Once or twice he fancied he heard a distant laugh, and the sound of voices singing drunkenly somewhere in the open air.

Some distance up the street a tall liberty-pole sustaining a swinging sign announced a tavern. Lynde hastened thither; but the tavern, like the private houses, appeared tenantless; the massive pine window-shutters were barred and bolted. Lynde mounted the three or four low steps leading to the piazza, and tried the front door, which was locked. With the saddle still on his shoulders, he stepped into the middle of the street to reconnoitre the premises. A man and two women suddenly showed themselves at an open window in the second story. Lynde was about to address them when the man cried out—

"Oh, you're a horse, I suppose. Well, there isn't any oats for you here. You had better trot on!"

Lynde did not relish this pleasantry; it struck him as rather insolent; but he curbed his irritation, and inquired as politely as he could if a horse or any kind of vehicle could be hired in the village.

The three persons in the window nodded to one another significantly, and began smiling in a constrained manner, as if there were something quite preposterous in the inquiry. The man, a corpulent, red-faced person, seemed on the point of suffocating with merriment.

"Is this a public house?" demanded Lynde severely.

"That's as may be," answered the man, recovering his breath, and becoming grave.

"Are you the proprietor?"

"That's jest what I am."

"Then I require of you the accommodation which is the right of every traveller. Your license does not permit you to turn any respectable stranger from your door."

"Now, my advice to you," said the man, stepping back from the window, "my advice to you is to trot. You can't get in here. If you try to, I'll pepper you as sure as you live, though I wouldn't like to do it. So trot right along!"

The man had a gun in his hands; he clutched it nervously by the stock; his countenance worked strangely, and his small, greenish eyes had a terrified, defiant expression. Indisputably, the tavern-keeper looked upon Lynde as a dangerous person, and was ready to fire upon him if he persisted in his demands.

"My friend," said Lynde through his set teeth, "if I had you down here I'd give you a short lesson in manners."

"I dare say! I dare say!" cried the man, flourishing the shot-gun excitedly.

Lynde turned away disgusted and indignant; but his indignation was neutralized by his astonishment at this incomprehensible brutality. He had no resource but to apply to some private house and state his predicament. As that luckless saddle had excited the derision of the girl, and drawn down on him the contumely of the tavern-keeper, he looked around for some safe spot in which to deposit it before it brought him into further disgrace. His linen and all his worldly possessions, except his money, which he carried on his person, were in the valise; he could not afford to lose that.

The sun was high by this time, and the heat would have been intolerable if it had not been for a merciful breeze which swept down from the cooler atmosphere of the hills. Lynde wasted half an hour or more seeking a hiding-place for the saddle. It had grown a grievous burden to him; at every step it added a pound to its dead weight. He saw no way of relieving himself of it. There it was perched upon his shoulders, like the Old Man of the Sea on the back of Sindbad the Sailor. In sheer despair Lynde flung down his load on the curb-stone at a corner formed by a narrow street diagonally crossing the main thoroughfare, which he had not quitted. He drew out his handkerchief and wiped the heavy drops of perspiration from his brows. At that moment he was aware of the presence of a tall, cadaverous man of about forty, who was so painfully pinched and emaciated that a sympathetic shiver ran over Lynde as he glanced at him. He was as thin as an exclamation point. It seemed to Lynde that the man must be perishing with cold even in that burning June sunshine. It was not a man, but a skeleton.

"Good heavens, sir!" cried Lynde. "Tell me where I am! What is the name of this town?"

"Constantinople."

"Constan"—

"—tinople," added the man briskly. "A stranger here?"

"Yes," said Lynde abstractedly. He was busy running over an imaginary map of the State of New Hampshire in search of Constantinople.

"Good!" exclaimed the anatomy, rustling his dry palms together, "I'll employ you."

"You'll employ me? I like that!"

"Certainly. I'm a ship-builder."

"I didn't know they built vessels a hundred miles from the coast," said Lynde.

"I am building a ship—don't say I'm not!"

"Of course I know nothing about it."

"A marble ship."

"A ship to carry marble?"

"No, a ship made of marble; a passenger ship. We have ships of iron, why not of marble?" he asked fiercely.

"Oh, the fellow is mad!" said Lynde to himself, "as mad as a loon; everybody here is mad, or I've lost my senses. So you are building a marble ship?" he added aloud, good-naturedly. "When it is finished I trust you will get all the inhabitants of this town into it, and put to sea at once."

"Then you'll help me!" cried the man enthusiastically, with his eyes gleaming in their sunken sockets. More than ever he looked like a specimen escaped from some anatomical museum.

"I do not believe I can be of much assistance," answered Lynde, laughing. "I have had so little experience in constructing marble vessels, you see. I fear my early education has been fearfully neglected. By the bye," continued the young man, who was vaguely diverted by his growing interest in the monomaniac, "how do you propose to move your ship to the seaboard?"

"In the simplest manner—a double railroad track—twenty-four engines—twelve engines on each side to support the hull."

"That WOULD be a simple way."

Edward Lynde laughed again, but not heartily. He felt that this marble ship was a conception of high humor and was not without its pathetic element. The whimsicality of the idea amused him, but the sad earnestness of the nervous, unstrung visionary at his side moved his compassion.

"Dear me," he mused, "may be all of us are more or less engaged in planning a marble ship, and perhaps the happiest are those who, like this poor soul, never awake from their delusion. Matrimony was uncle David's marble ship— he launched his! Have I one on the ways, I wonder?"

Lynde broke with a shock from his brief abstraction. His companion had disappeared, and with him the saddle and valise. Lynde threw a hasty glance up the street, and started in pursuit of the naval-architect, who was running with incredible swiftness and bearing the saddle on his head with as much ease as if it had been a feather.

The distance between the two men, some sixty or seventy yards, was not the disadvantage that made pursuit seem hopeless. Lynde had eaten almost nothing since the previous noon; he had been carrying that cumbersome saddle for the last two or three hours; he was out of breath, and it was impossible to do much running in his heavy riding-boots. The other man, on the contrary, appeared perfectly fresh; he wore light shoes, and had not a superfluous ounce of flesh to carry. He was all bone and sinew; the saddle resting upon his head was hardly an impediment to him. Lynde, however, was not going to be vanquished without a struggle; though he recognized the futility of pursuit, he pushed on doggedly. A certain tenacious quality in the young man imperatively demanded this of him.

"The rascal has made off with my dinner," he muttered between his clinched teeth. "That completes the ruin Mary began. If I should happen to catch up with him, I trust I shall have the moral strength not to knock his head off— his skull off; it isn't a head."

Lynde's sole hope of overtaking him, and it was a very slender hope, was based on the possibility that the man might fall and disable himself; but he seemed to have the sure-footedness as well as the lightness of a deer. When Lynde reached the outskirts of the village, on the road by which he had entered, the agile ship-builder was more than halfway up the hill. Lynde made a fresh spurt here, and lost his hat; but he had no time to turn back for it. Every instant widened the space between the two runners, as one of them noticed with disgust. At the top of the ascent the man halted a moment to take breath, and then disappeared behind the ridge. He was on the down grade now, and of course gaining at each stride on his pursuer, who was still toiling upward. Lynde did not slacken his pace, however; he had got what runners call their second wind. With lips set, elbows pressed against his sides, and head thrown forward, he made excellent time to the brow of the hill, where he suddenly discovered himself in the midst of a crowd of men and horses.

For several seconds Lynde was so dazed and embarrassed that he saw nothing; then his eyes fell upon the girl with the long hair and the white gown. She was seated sidewise on a horse without saddle, and the horse was Mary. A strapping fellow was holding the animal by the head-stall.

"By Jove!" cried Lynde, springing forward joyfully, "that's my mare!"

He was immediately seized by two men who attempted to pass a cord over his wrists. Lynde resisted so desperately that a third man was called into requisition, and the three succeeded in tying his hands and placing him upon a saddle vacated by one of the riders. All this occupied hardly a minute.

"Will you go along quietly," said one of the men roughly, "or will you be carried?"

"What is the meaning of this?" demanded Lynde, with the veins standing out on his forehead.

He received no reply from any of the group, which seemed to be composed of farmers and laboring-hands, with two or three persons whose social status did not betray itself. Directly behind the girl and, like her, mounted on a horse led by a couple of rustics, was the white-haired old gentleman who had repulsed Lynde so rudely. Lynde noticed that his hands were also secured by cords, an indignity which in no wise altered the benevolent and satisfied expression of his face. Lynde's saddle and valise were attached to the old gentleman's horse. Lynde instinctively looked around for the ship-builder. There he was, flushed and sullen, sitting on a black nag as bony and woe-begone as himself, guarded by two ill-favored fellows. Not only were the ship-builder's arms pinioned, but his feet were bound by a rope fastened to each ankle and passed under the nag's belly. It was clear to Lynde that he himself, the old clergyman, and the girl were the victims of some dreadful misconception, possibly brought about by the wretch who had purloined the saddle.

"Gentlemen!" cried Lynde, as the party began to advance, "I protest against this outrage so far as I am concerned, and I venture to protest on the part of the lady. I am convinced that she is incapable of any act to warrant such treatment. I—I know her slightly," he added, hesitating.

"Oh, yes," said the girl, folding her hands demurely in her lap, "and I know you, too, very well. You are my husband."

This announcement struck Lynde speechless. The rough men exchanged amused glances, and the ship-builder gave vent to a curious dry laugh. Lynde could have killed him. The party moved on. Up to this moment the young man had been boiling with rage; his rage now yielded place to amazement. What motive had prompted the girl to claim that relationship? Was it a desperate appeal to him for protection? But brother, or cousin, or friend would have served as well. Her impulsive declaration, which would be at once disproved, might result in serious complications for him and her. But it had not been an impulsive declaration; she had said it very calmly, and, he fancied, with just the lightest touch of coquetry, "You are my husband!" For several minutes Lynde did not dare to let his eyes wander in her direction. She was a pace or so in the rear at his right. To see her he would be obliged to turn slightly; this he presently did, with a movement as if settling himself more easily in the saddle. The girl's loose hair was blown like a black veil over her face, putting her into mourning; she was steadying herself with one hand resting on Mary's mane; her feet were crossed, and a diminutive slipper had fallen from one of them. There was something so helpless and appealing in the girl's attitude that Lynde was touched.

"May I speak with you, sir?" he said, addressing himself to a man whom somebody had called Morton, and who appeared to issue the orders for the party. The man came to Lynde's side.

"For Heaven's sake, sir, explain this! Who is that young woman?"

"You said you knew her," returned the man, not unpleasantly.

"Indeed I said so," replied Lynde, reddening. "What has happened? What has she done, what have I done, what has the old clergyman done, that we should be seized like murderers on the public highway?"

"Be quiet now," said the man, laying his hand soothingly on Lynde's arm, and looking at him steadily. "Everything will be satisfactorily explained by and by."

Lynde's indignation blazed up again.

"I can assure you, sir," he cried, as the man returned to his former position, "that the result of the explanation will be far from satisfactory to you. I shall hold to strict account every man who has had a hand in this business. I demand to be brought before a magistrate, or a justice of the peace, if there is one in this God-forsaken country."

No attention was paid to Lynde's fresh outbreak. Some one picked up his hat and set it on the back of his head, giving him quite a rakish air. His dignity suffered until the wind took the hat again. The party proceeded in silence, halting once to tighten a girth, and another time to wait for a straggler. If the men spoke to one another it was in subdued tones or whispers. Two of the horsemen trotted on a hundred yards in advance, like skirmishers thrown out in front of an attacking force. There was something in all this mysterious precaution and reticence which bewildered and exasperated Lynde, who noted every detail. Mary, in a transient spasm of backing, had fallen to the rear; the young man could no longer see the girl, but ever before his eyes was the piteous, unslippered little foot with its arched instep.

The party was now at the base of the declivity. Instead of following the road to the village, the horses turned abruptly into a bridle-path branching off to the left, and in the course of a few minutes passed through an iron-spiked gateway in a high brick wall surrounding the large red structure which had puzzled Lynde on first discovering the town. The double gates stood wide open and were untended; they went to, however, with a clang, and the massive bolts were shot as soon as the party had entered. In the courtyard Lynde was hastily assisted from the horse; he did not have an opportunity to observe what became of the other three prisoners. When his hands were freed he docilely allowed himself to be conducted up a flight of stone steps and into the vestibule of the building, and thence, through a long corridor, to a small room in which his guard left him. The door closed with a spring not practicable from the inside, as Lynde ascertained on inspection.

The chamber was not exactly a cell; it resembled rather the waiting-room of a penitentiary. The carpet, of a tasteless, gaudy pattern, was well worn, and the few pieces of hair-cloth furniture, a sofa, a table, and chairs, had a stiff, official air. A strongly barred window gave upon a contracted garden—one of those gardens sometimes attached to prisons, with mathematically cut box borders, and squares of unhealthy, party-colored flowers looking like gangs of convicts going to meals. On his arrival at the place Edward Lynde had offered no resistance, trusting that some sort of judicial examination would promptly set him at liberty. Faint from want of food, jaded by his exertions, and chafing at the delay, he threw himself upon the sofa, and waited.

There was a great deal of confusion in the building. Hurried footsteps came and went up and down the passages; now and then he heard approaching voices, which tantalizingly passed on, or died away before reaching his door. Once a shrill shriek—a woman's shriek—rang through the corridor and caused him to spring to his feet.

After the lapse of an hour that had given Lynde some general idea of eternity, the door was hastily thrown open, and a small, elderly, blue-eyed gentleman, followed by a man of gigantic stature, entered the chamber.

"My dear sir," cried the gentleman, making a courteous, deprecatory gesture with his palms spread outward, "we owe you a million apologies. There has been a most lamentable mistake!"

"A mistake!" said Lynde haughtily. "Mistake is a mild term to apply to an outrage."

"Your indignation is just; still it was a mistake, and one I would not have had happen for the world. I am Dr. Pendegrast, the superintendent of this asylum."

"This is an asylum!"

"An asylum for the insane," returned Dr. Pendegrast. "I do not know how to express my regret at what has occurred. I can only account for the unfortunate affair, and throw myself upon your generosity. Will you allow me to explain?"

Lynde passed his hand over his forehead in a bewildered way. Then he looked at the doctor suspiciously; Lynde's late experience had shaken his faith in the general sanity of his species. "Certainly," he said, "I would like to have this matter explained to me; for I'll be hanged if I understand it. This is an asylum?"

"Yes, sir."

"And you are the superintendent?"

"Yes, sir."

"Then—naturally—you are not a lunatic?"

"Certainly not!" said the doctor, starting.

"Very well; I didn't know. I am listening to you, sir."

"Early this morning," said Dr. Pendegrast, somewhat embarrassed by Lynde's singular manner, "a number of patients whom we had always considered tractable seized the attendants one by one at breakfast, and, before a general alarm could be given, locked them in the cells. Some of us were still in our bedrooms when the assault began and were there overpowered. We chanced to be short-handed at the time, two of the attendants being ill, and another absent. As I say, we were all seized—the women attendants and nurses as well—and locked up. Higgins here, my head-man, they put into a strait-jacket."

"Yes, sir," spoke up Higgins for himself, "they did so!"

"Me," continued Dr. Pendegrast, smiling, "they confined in the padded chamber."

Lynde looked at him blankly.

"A chamber with walls thickly cushioned, to prevent violent patients from inflicting injury on themselves," explained the doctor. "*I*, you see, was considered a very bad case indeed! Meanwhile, Morton, the under-keeper, was in the garden, and escaped; but unfortunately, in his excitement, he neglected to lock the main gate after him. Morton gave the alarm to the people in the village, who, I am constrained to say, did not behave handsomely. Instead of coming to our relief and assisting to restore order, which might easily have been done even then, they barricaded themselves in their houses, in a panic. Morton managed to get a horse, and started for G—In the meantime the patients who had made the attack liberated the patients still in confinement, and the whole rushed in a body out of the asylum and spread themselves over the village."

"That must have been the crowd I saw in the streets when I sighted the town," said Lynde, thinking aloud.

"If you saw persons in the street," returned the doctor, "they were not the townsfolk. They kept very snug, I assure you. But permit me to finish, Mr."—

"My name is Lynde."

"Morton," continued the doctor, bowing, "having secured several volunteers before reaching G—, decided to return with what force he had, knowing that every instant was precious. On his way back he picked up three of the poor wanderers, and, unluckily, picked up you."

"He should not have committed such a stupid error," said Lynde, clinging stoutly to his grievance. "He ought to have seen that I was not an inmate of the asylum."

"An attendant, my dear Mr. Lynde, is not necessarily familiar with all the patients; he may know only those in his special ward. Besides, you were bare-headed and running, and seemed in a state of great cerebral excitement."

"I was chasing a man who had stolen my property."

"Morton and the others report that you behaved with great violence."

"Of course I did. I naturally resented being seized and bound."

"Your natural violence confirmed them in their natural suspicion, you see. Assuredly they were to blame; but the peculiar circumstances must plead for them."

"But when I spoke to them calmly and rationally"—

"My good sir," interrupted the doctor, "if sane people always talked as rationally and sensibly as some of the very maddest of my poor friends sometimes do, there would be fewer foolish things said in the world. What remark is that the great poet puts into the mouth of Polonius, speaking of Hamlet? 'How pregnant sometimes his replies are! a happiness that often madness hits on, which reason and sanity could not so prosperously be delivered of.' My dear Mr. Lynde, it was your excellent good sense that convicted you! By the way, I believe you claimed the horse which Morton found adrift on the road."

"Yes, sir, it was mine; at least I was riding it this morning when the saddle-girth broke, and the mare got away from me."

"Then of course that was your saddle Blaisdell was running off with."

"Blaisdell?"

"One of our most dangerous patients, in fact, the only really dangerous patient at present in the establishment. Yet you should hear HIM talk sometimes! To-day, thank God, he happened to be in his ship-building mood. Otherwise—I dare not think what he might have done. I should be in despair if he had not been immediately retaken. Oddly enough, all the poor creatures, except three, returned to the asylum of their own will, after a brief ramble through the village."

"And the white-haired old gentleman who looked like a clergyman, is he mad?"

"Mackenzie? Merely idiotic," replied the doctor, with the cool professional air.

"And the young girl," asked Lynde hesitatingly, "is she"—

"A very sad case," interrupted Dr. Pendegrast, with a tenderer expression settling upon his countenance. "The saddest thing in the world."

"Insane?"

"Hopelessly so, I fear."

A nameless heaviness fell upon Lynde's heart. He longed to ask other questions, but he did not know how to shape them. He regretted that subsequently.

"And now, Mr. Lynde," said the doctor, "in your general pardon I wish you to include my unavoidable delay in coming or sending to you. When you were brought here I was still in durance vile, and Higgins was in his strait-jacket. On being released, my hands were full, as you can suppose. Moreover, I did not learn at once of your detention. The saddle and the valise caused me to suspect that a blunder had been committed. I cannot adequately express my regrets. In ten minutes," continued Dr. Pendegrast, turning a fat gold watch over on its back in the palm of his hand, where it looked like a little yellow turtle, "in ten minutes dinner will be served. Unless you do me the honor to dine with me, I shall not believe in the sincerity of your forgiveness."

"Thanks," said Lynde dejectedly. "I fully appreciate your thoughtfulness; I am nearly famished, but I do not think I could eat a mouthful here. Excuse me for saying it, but I should have to remain here permanently if I were to stay another hour. I quite forgive Mr. Morton and the others," Lynde went on, rising and giving the doctor his hand; "and I forgive you also, since you insist upon being forgiven, though I do not know for what. If my horse, and my traps, and my hat—really, I don't see how they could have helped taking me for a lunatic—can be brought together, I will go and dine at the tavern."

Half an hour afterward Edward Lynde dismounted at the steps of the rustic hotel. The wooden shutters were down now, and the front door stood hospitably open. A change had come over the entire village. There were knots of persons at the street corners and at garden gates, discussing the event of the day. There was also a knot of gossips in the hotel barroom to whom the landlord, Mr. Zeno Dodge, was giving a thrilling account of an attack made on the tavern by a maniac who had fancied himself a horse!

"The critter," cried Mr. Dodge dramatically, "was on the p'int of springin' up the piazzy, when Martha handed me the shot-gun."

Mr. Dodge was still in a heroic attitude, with one arm stretched out to receive the weapon and his eye following every movement of a maniac obligingly personated by the cuspidor between the windows, when Lynde entered. Mr. Dodge's arm slowly descended to his side, his jaw fell, and the narrative broke off short.

Lynde requested dinner in a private room, and Mr. Dodge deposed the maid in order to bring in the dishes himself and scrutinize his enigmatical guest.

In serving the meal the landlord invented countless pretexts to remain in the room. After a while Lynde began to feel it uncomfortable to have those sharp green eyes continually boring into the back of his head.

"Yes," he exclaimed wearily, "I am the man."

"I thought you was. Glad to see you, sir," said Mr. Dodge politely.

"This morning you took me for an escaped lunatic?"

"I did so—fust-off."

"A madman who imagined himself a horse?"

"That's what I done," said Mr. Dodge contritely, "an' no wonder, with that there saddle. They're a very queer lot, them crazy chaps. There's one on 'em up there who calls himself Abraham Lincoln, an' then there's another who thinks he's a telegraph wire an' hes messages runnin' up an' down him continally. These is new potatoes, sir—early rosers. There's no end to their cussed kinks. When I see you prancin' round under the winder with that there saddle, I says at once to Martha, 'Martha, here's a luny!'"

"A very natural conclusion," said Lynde meekly.

"Wasn't it now?"

"And if you had shot me to death," said Lynde, helping himself to another chop, "I should have been very much obliged to you."

Mr. Dodge eyed the young man dubiously for a dozen seconds or so.

"Comin'! comin'!" cried Mr. Dodge, in response to a seemingly vociferous call which had failed to reach Lynde's ear.

When Edward Lynde had finished dinner, Mary was brought to the door. Under the supervision of a group of spectators assembled on the piazza, Lynde mounted, and turned the mare's head directly for Rivermouth. He had no heart to go any farther due north. The joyousness had dropped out of the idle summer journey. He had gone in search of the picturesque and the peculiar; he had found them—and he wished he had not.

V

CINDERELLA'S SLIPPER

On the comb of the hill where his adventure had begun and culminated—it seemed to him now like historic ground—Edward Lynde reined in Mary, to take a parting look at the village nestled in the plain below. Already the afternoon light was withdrawing from the glossy chestnuts and drooping elms, and the twilight—it crept into the valley earlier than elsewhere—was weaving its half invisible webs under the eaves and about the gables of the houses. But the two red towers of the asylum reached up into the mellow radiance of the waning sun, and stood forth boldly. They were the last objects his gaze rested upon, and to them alone his eyes sent a farewell.

"Poor little thing! poor little Queen of Sheba!" he said softly. Then the ridge rose between him and the village, and shut him out forever.

Nearly a mile beyond the spot where Mary had escaped from him that morning, Edward Lynde drew up the mare so sharply that she sunk back on her haunches. He dismounted in haste, and stooping down, with the rein thrown over one arm, picked up an object lying in the middle of the road under the horse's very hoofs.

It was on a Tuesday morning that Lynde reentered Rivermouth, after an absence of just eight days. He had started out fresh and crisp as a new bank-note, and came back rumpled and soiled and tattered, like that same note in a state to be withdrawn from circulation. The shutters were up at all the shop-windows in the cobble-paved street, and had the appearance of not having been taken down since he left. Everything was unchanged, yet it seemed to Lynde that he had been gone a year.

On Wednesday morning when Mr. Bowlsby came down to the bank he was slightly surprised at seeing the young cashier at his accustomed desk. To Mr. Bowlsby's brief interrogations then, and to Miss Mildred Bowlsby's more categorical questions in the evening, Lynde offered no very lucid reason for curtailing his vacation. Travelling alone had not been as pleasant as he anticipated; the horse was a nuisance to look after; and then the country taverns were snuffy and unendurable. As to where he had been and what he had seen—he must have seen something and been somewhere in eight days—his answers were so evasive that Miss Mildred was positive something distractingly romantic had befallen the young man.

"If you must know," he said, one evening, "I will tell you where I went."

"Tell me, then!"

"I went to Constantinople."

Miss Mildred found that nearly impertinent.

There was, too, an alteration in Lynde's manner which cruelly helped to pique her curiosity. His frank, half satirical, but wholly amiable way—an armor that had hitherto rendered him invulnerable to Miss Mildred's coquettish shafts—was wanting; he was less ready to laugh than formerly, and sometimes in the midst of company he fell into absent-minded moods. Instead of being the instigator and leader of picnics up the river, he frequently pleaded bank duties as an excuse for not joining such parties. "He is not at all as nice as he used to be," was Miss Mildred's mental summing up of Lynde a fortnight after his return.

He was, in fact, unaccountably depressed by his adventure in the hill country; he could not get it out of his mind. The recollection of details which he had not especially remarked at the time came to him in the midst of his work at the bank. Sometimes when he turned off the gas at night, or just as he was falling asleep, the sharp, attenuated figure of the ship-builder limned itself against the blackness of the chamber, or the old gentleman's vacuous countenance in its frame of silver hair peered in through the hangings of the bed. But more frequently it was the young girl's face that haunted Lynde. He saw her as she came up the sunny road, swinging the flower in her hand, and looking like one of Fra Angelico's seraphs or some saint out of an illuminated mediaeval missal; then he saw her seated on the horse, helpless and piteous with the rude, staring men about her. If he dreamed, it was of her drawing herself up haughtily and saying, "I am the Queen of Sheba." On two or three nights, when he had not been dreaming, he was startled out of his slumber by a voice whispering close to his ear: "I know you, too, very well. You are my husband."

Mr. Bowlsby and his daughter were the only persons in Rivermouth to whom Lynde could have told the story of his journey. He decided not to confide it to either, since he felt it would be vain to attempt to explain the sombre effect which the whole affair had had on him.

"I do not understand what makes me think of that poor girl all the time," mused Lynde one day, as he stood by the writing-table in his sitting-room. "It can't be this that keeps her in my mind."

He took up a slipper which was lying on the table in the midst of carved pipes and paper-weights and odds and ends. It was a very small slipper, nearly new, with high pointed heel and a square jet buckle at the instep: evidently of foreign make, and cut after the arch pattern of the slippers we see peeping from the flowered brocade skirts of Sir Peter Lely's full-length ladies. It was such an absurd shoe, a toy shoe, a child might have worn it!

"It cannot be this," said Lynde.

And yet it was that, more or less. Lynde had taken the slipper from his valise the evening he got home, and set it on the corner of the desk, where it straightway made itself into a cunning ornament. The next morning he put it into one of the drawers; but the table looked so barren and commonplace without it that presently the thing was back again. There it had remained ever since.

It met his eye every morning when he opened the door of his bedroom; it was there when he came home late at night, and seemed to be sitting up for him, in the reproachful, feminine fashion. When he was writing his letters, there it was, with a prim, furtive air of looking on. It was not like a mere slipper; it had traits and an individuality of its own; there were moments when the jet beads in the buckle sparkled with a sort of intelligence. Sitting at night, reading under the drop-light, Lynde often had an odd sensation as if the little shoe would presently come tripping across the green table-cloth towards him. He had a hundred fanciful humors growing out of that slipper. Sometimes he was tempted to lock it up or throw it away. Sometimes he would say to himself, half mockingly and half sadly, "That is your wife's slipper;" then he would turn wholly sad, thinking how tragic that would be if it were really so.

It was a part of the girl's self; it had borne her lovely weight; it still held the impress of her foot; it would not let Lynde entirely forget her while it was under his eyes.

The slipper had stood on the writing-table four or five months—an object of consuming curiosity and speculation to the young woman who dusted Lynde's chambers—when an incident occurred which finally led to its banishment.

Lynde never had visitors; there were few men of his age in the town, and none was sufficiently intimate with him to come to his rooms; but it chanced one evening that a young man named Preston dropped in to smoke a cigar with Lynde. Preston had recently returned from abroad, where he had been an attache of the American Legation at London, and was now generally regarded as the prospective proprietor of Miss Mildred. He was an entertaining, mercurial young fellow, into whose acquaintanceship Lynde had fallen at the Bowlsbys'.

"Ah, you rogue!" cried Preston gayly, picking up the slipper. "Did she give it you?"

"Who?" asked Lynde, with a start.

"Devilish snug little foot! Was it a danseuse?"

"No," returned Lynde freezingly.

"An actress?"

"No," said Lynde, taking the slipper from Preston's hand and gently setting it back on the writing-table. "It was not an actress; and yet she played a role— in a blacker tragedy than any you ever saw on the stage."

"Lynde, I beg your pardon. I spoke thoughtlessly, supposing it a light matter, don't you see?"

"There was no offence," said Lynde, hiding his subtile hurt.

"It was stupid in me," said Preston the next night, relating the incident to Miss Bowlsby. "I never once thought it might be a thing connected with the memory of his mother or sister, don't you see? I took it for a half sentimental souvenir of some flirtation."

"Mr. Lynde's mother died when he was a child, and he never had a sister," said Miss Bowlsby thoughtfully. "I shouldn't wonder," she added irrelevantly, after a pause.

"At what, Miss Mildred?"

"At anything!"

One of those womanly intuitions which set mere man-logic at defiance was come to whisper in Miss Bowlsby's ear that that slipper had performed some part in Edward Lynde's untold summer experience.

"He was laughing at you, Mr. Preston; he was grossly imposing on your unsophisticated innocence."

"Really? Is he as deep as that?"

"He is very deep," said Miss Bowlsby solemnly.

On his way home from the bank, one afternoon in that same week, Lynde overtook Miss Mildred walking, and accompanied her a piece down the street.

"Mr. Lynde, shall you go on another horseback excursion next summer?" she asked, without prelude.

"I haven't decided; but I think not."

"Of course you ought to go."

"Why of course, Miss Mildred?"

"Why? Because—because—don't ask me!"

"But I do ask you."

"You insist?"

"Positively."

"Well, then, how will you ever return Cinderella her slipper if you don't go in search of her?"

Lynde bit his lip, and felt that the blackest criminals of antiquity were as white as driven snow compared with Preston.

"The prince in the story, you know," continued Miss Bowlsby, with her smile of ingenue, "hunted high and low until he found her again."

"That prince was a very energetic fellow," said Lynde, hastily putting on his old light armor. "Possibly I should not have to travel so far from home," he added, with a bow. "I know at least one lady in Rivermouth who has a Cinderella foot."

"She has two of them, Mr. Lynde," responded Miss Mildred, dropping him a courtesy.

The poor little slipper's doom was sealed. The edict for its banishment had gone forth. If it were going to be the town's talk he could not keep it on his writing-desk. As soon as Lynde got back to his chambers, he locked up Cinderella's slipper in an old trunk in a closet seldom or never opened.

The enchantment, whatever it was, was broken. Although he missed the slipper from among the trifles scattered over his table, its absence brought him a kind of relief. He less frequently caught himself falling into brown studies. The details of his adventure daily grew more indistinct; the picture was becoming a mere outline; it was fading away. He might have been able in the course of time to set the whole occurrence down as a grotesque dream, if he had not now and then beheld Deacon Twombly driving by the bank with Mary attached to the battered family carry-all. Mary was a fact not easily disposed of.

Insensibly Lynde lapsed into his old habits. The latter part of this winter at Rivermouth was unusually gay; the series of evening parties and lectures and private theatricals extended into the spring, whose advent was signalized by the marriage of Miss Bowlsby and Preston. In June Lynde ran on to New York for a week, where he had a clandestine dinner with his uncle at Delmonico's, and bade good-by to Flemming, who was on the eve of starting on a protracted tour through the East. "I shall make it a point to visit the land of the Sabaeans," said Flemming, with his great cheery laugh, "and discover, if possible, the unknown site of the ancient capital of Sheba." Lynde had confided the story to his friend one night, coming home from the theatre.

Once more at Rivermouth, Edward Lynde took up the golden threads of his easy existence. But this life of ideal tranquillity and contentment was not to be permitted him. One morning in the latter part of August he received a letter advising him that his uncle had had an alarming stroke of apoplexy. The letter was followed within the hour by a telegram announcing the death of David Lynde.

VI

BEYOND THE SEA

In the early twilight of a July evening in the year 1875, two young Americans, neither dreaming of the other's presence, came face to face on the steps of a hotel on the Quai du Montblanc at Geneva. The two men, one of whom was so bronzed by Eastern suns that his friend looked pallid beside him, exchanged a long, incredulous stare; then their hands met, and the elder cried out, "Of all men in the world!"

"Flemming!" exclaimed the other eagerly; "I thought you were in Egypt."

"So I was, a month ago. What are you doing over here, Ned?"

"I don't know, to tell the truth."

"You don't know!" laughed Flemming. "Enjoying yourself, I suppose."

"The supposition is a little rash," said Edward Lynde. "I have been over nearly a year—quite a year, in fact. After uncle David's death"—

"Poor old fellow! I got the news at Smyrna."

"After he was gone, and the business of the estate was settled, I turned restless at Rivermouth. It was cursedly lonesome. I hung on there awhile, and then I came abroad."

"A rich man—my father wrote me. I have had no letter's from you. Your uncle treated you generously, Ned."

"Did he not always treat me generously?" said Lynde, with a light coming into his face and instantly dying out again. "Yes, he left me a pile of money and a heart-ache. I can hardly bear to talk of it even now, and it will be two years this August. But come up to my room. By Jove, I am glad to see you! How is it you are in Geneva? I was thinking about you yesterday, and wondering whether you were drifting down the Nile in a dahabeeah, or crossing the desert on a dromedary. Of course you have hunted tigers and elephants: did you kill anything?"

"I haven't killed anything but time. I was always a dead shot at that."

Lynde passed his arm through Flemming's, and the two friends mounted the staircase of the hotel.

"How is it you are in Geneva?" repeated Lynde.

"By luck," answered Flemming. "I am going home—in a zigzag way. I've been obliged to take a reef in my Eastern itinerary. The fact is, I have had a letter from the old gentleman rather suggesting it. I believe he has availed himself of my absence to fall into financial difficulties."

"Why, I thought he was rolling in wealth."

"No, he is rolling in poverty, as nearly as I can make out. Well, not so bad as that. Nothing is ever as bad as it pretends to be. But he has met with heavy losses. I shall find letters in London and learn all about it. He wrote me not to hurry, that a month or two would make no difference. When I got to Munich I thought I would take a peep at Switzerland while I had the opportunity. I have done a good piece—from Lindau to Lucerne, from Lucerne to Martigny by way of the Furca; through the Tete Noire Pass to Chamouni, and from Chamouni, here."

While Flemming was speaking, Lynde unlocked a door at the end of the hall and ushered him into a sitting-room with three windows, each opening upon a narrow balcony of its own.

"Sit there, old fellow," said Lynde, wheeling an easy-chair to the middle window, "and look through my glass at the view before it takes itself off. It is not often as fine as it is this evening."

In front of the hotel the blue waters of the Rhone swept under the arches of the Pont des Bergues, to lose themselves in the turbid, glacier-born Arve, a mile below the town. Between the Pont des Bergues and the Pont du Montblanc lay the island of Jean Jacques Rousseau, linked to the quay by a tiny chain bridge. Opposite, upon the right bank of the Rhone, stretched the handsome facades of tile-roofed buildings, giving one an idea of the ancient quarter which a closer inspection dispels; for the streets are crooked and steep, and the houses, except those lining the quays, squalid. It was not there, however, that the eye would have lingered. Far away, seen an incredible distance in the transparent evening atmosphere, Mont Blanc and its massed group of snowy satellites lifted themselves into the clouds. All those luminous battlements and turrets and pyramids—the Mole, the Grandes Jorasses, the Aiguilles du Midi, the Dent du Geant, the Aiguilles d'Argentiere—were now suffused with a glow so magically delicate that the softest tint of the blush rose would have seemed harsh and crude in comparison.

"You have to come away from Mont Blanc to see it," said Flemming, lowering the glass. "When I had my nose against it at Chamouni I didn't see it at all. It overhung me and smothered me. Old boy"—reaching up his hand to Lynde who was leaning on the back of the chair—"who would ever have thought that we two"—Flemming stopped short and looked earnestly into his comrade's face. "Why, Ned, I didn't notice how thin and pale you are. Are you ill?"

The color which had mantled Lynde's cheeks in the first surprise and pleasure of meeting his friend had passed away, leaving, indeed, a somewhat haggard expression on the young man's countenance.

"Ill? Not that I know."

"Is anything wrong?"

"There is nothing wrong," replied Lynde, with some constraint. "That is to say, nothing very wrong. For a month or six weeks I have been occupied with a matter that has rather unsettled me—more, perhaps, than I ought to have allowed."

"What is that?"

"It doesn't signify. Don't let's speak of it."

"But it does signify. You are keeping something serious from me. Out with it."

"Well, the truth is," said Lynde after a moment's hesitation, "it IS something serious and nothing very positive: that's the perplexing part of it."

"You are not making it clear to me."

"I don't know that I can, Flemming."

"Try, then."

Lynde reflected a few seconds, with his eyes fixed on the remote mountain lines imperceptibly melting into the twilight. "Do you remember our walk home from the theatre, one night, two or three days before you sailed from New York?"

"Perfectly," replied Flemming.

"Do you recollect my telling you of a queer thing that happened to me up in the New Hampshire hills?"

"Your encounter with the little lunatic? Perfectly."

"Don't!" said Lynde, shrinking as if some sharp instrument had pierced him. "She is here!"

"Here!" exclaimed Flemming, half rising from the chair, and glancing towards a draped door which connected the suite of apartments.

"Not in these rooms," said Lynde, with a short laugh, "but in Geneva—in this hotel."

"You do not mean it."

"When I say it is she, I'm not sure of it."

"Of course it isn't."

"That's what I say, and the next moment I know it is."

"And is THIS your trouble?"

"Yes," answered Lynde, knitting his brows. "I felt that I shouldn't make it clear to you."

"I am afraid you haven't, Ned. What earthly difference does it make to you whether or not it's the same girl?"

"What difference!" cried Lynde impetuously; "what difference—when I love the very ground she walks on!"

"Oh, you love her! Which one?"

"Don't laugh at me, Flemming."

"I am not laughing," said Flemming, looking puzzled and anxious. "It is not possible, Ned, you have allowed yourself to go and get interested in a—a person not right in her mind!"

"Miss Denham is as sane as you are."

"Then Miss—Denham, is it?—cannot be the girl you told me about."

"That's the point."

"I don't see why there should be any confusion on that point."

"Don't you?"

"Come, let us go to the bottom of this. You have fallen in with a woman in Switzerland, and you suspect her of being a girl you met years ago in New Hampshire under circumstances which render her appearance here nearly an impossibility. As I am not a man of vivid imagination, that floors me. What makes you think them identical?"

"A startling personal resemblance, age, inflection of voice, manner, even a certain physical peculiarity—a scar."

"Then what makes you doubt?"

"Everything."

"Well, that's comprehensive, at all events."

"The very fact of her being here. The physician at the asylum said that that girl's malady was hopeless. Miss Denham has one of the clearest intellects I ever knew; she is a linguist, an accomplished musician, and, what is more rare, a girl who has moved a great deal in society, or, at least, has travelled a great deal, and has not ceased to be an unaffected, fresh, candid girl."

"An American?"

"Of course; didn't I say so?"

"The other may have been a sister, then, or a cousin," suggested Flemming. "That would account for the likeness, which possibly you exaggerate. It was in 1872, wasn't it?"

"I have been all over that. Miss Denham is an only child; she never had a cousin. To-day she is precisely what the other would have been, with restored health and three years added to her seventeen or eighteen."

"Upon my word, Ned, this is one of the oddest things I ever heard. I feel, though, that you have got yourself into an unnecessary snarl. Where does Miss Denham come from? She is not travelling alone? How did you meet her? Tell me the entire story."

"There is nothing to tell, or next to nothing. I met the Denhams here, six weeks ago. It was at the table d'hote. Two ladies came in and took places opposite me—a middle-aged lady and a young one. I did not notice them until they were seated; it was the voice of the younger lady that attracted me; I looked up,—and there was the Queen of Sheba. The same eyes, the same hair, the same face, though not so pale, and fuller; the same form, only the contours filled out. I put down my knife and fork and stared at her. She flushed, for I fancy I stared at her rather rudely, and a faint mark, like a star, came into her cheek and faded. I saw it as distinctly as I saw it the day she passed me on the country road, swinging the flower in her hand."

"By Jove! it's a regular romance—strawberry mark and all."

"If you don't take this seriously," said Lynde, frowning, "I am done."

"Go on."

"I shall never know how I got through the endless courses of that dinner; it was an empty pantomime on my part. As soon as it was over I rushed to the hotel register. The only entry among the new arrivals which pointed to the two ladies was that of Mrs. William Denham and Niece, United States. You can understand, Flemming, how I was seized with a desire to know those two women. I had come to Geneva for a day or so; but I resolved to stay here a month if they stayed, or to leave the next hour if they left. In short, I meant to follow them discreetly; it was an occupation for me. They remained. In the course of a week I knew the Denhams to speak to them when we met of a morning in the English Garden. A fortnight later it seemed to me that I had known them half my life. They had come across the previous November, they had wintered in Italy, and were going to Chamouni some time in July, where Mr. Denham was to join them; then they were to make an extended tour of Switzerland, accompanied by an old friend of the family, a professor, or a doctor, or something, who was in the south of France for his health. Miss Denham—her name is Ruth—is an orphan, and was educated mostly over here. When the Denhams are at home they live somewhere in the neighborhood of Orange, New Jersey. There are all the simple, exasperating facts. I can add nothing to them. If I were to tell you how this girl has perplexed and distressed me, by seeming to be and seeming not to be that other person—how my doubts and hopes have risen and fallen from day to day, even from hour to hour—it would be as uninteresting to you as a barometrical record. But this is certain: when Miss Denham and I part at Chamouni, as I suppose we shall, this world will have come to an end so far as I am concerned."

"The world doesn't come to an end that way—when one is twenty-six. Does she like you, Ned?"

"How can I say? She does not dislike me. We have seen very much of each other. We have been together some portion of each day for more than a month. But I've never had her a moment alone; the aunt is always present. We are like old friends—with a difference."

"I see; the aunt makes the difference! No flirting allowed on the premises."

"Miss Denham is not a girl to flirt with; she is very self-possessed, with just a suspicion of haughtiness; personally, tall, slight, a sort of dusky Eastern beauty, with the clear warm colors of a New England September twilight—not like the brunettes on this side, who are apt to have thick complexions, saving their presence. I say she is not a girl to flirt with, and yet, with that sensitive-cut mouth and those deep eyes, she could do awful things in the way of tenderness if she had a mind to. She's a puzzle, with her dove's innocence and her serpent's wisdom. All women are problems. I suppose every married man of us goes down to his grave with his particular problem not quite solved."

Flemming gave a loud laugh. The "every married man of us" tickled him. "Yes," said he; "they are all daughters of the Sphinx, and past finding out. Is Miss Denham an invalid?" he asked, after a pause.

"No; she is not strong—delicate, rather; of the pure type of American young-womanhood—more spirit than physique; but not an invalid—unless"—

"You have let a morbid fancy run away with you, Ned. This lady and the other one are two different persons."

"If I could only believe it!" said Lynde. "I do believe it at times; then some gesture, some fleeting expression, a turn of the head, the timbre of her voice—and there she is again! The next moment I am ready to laugh at myself."

"Couldn't you question the aunt?"

"How could I?"

"You couldn't!"

"I have thought of that doctor at the asylum—what in the devil was his name? I might write to him; but I shrink from doing it. I have been brutal enough in other ways. I am ashamed to confess to what unforgivable expedients I have resorted to solve my uncertainty. Once we were speaking of Genoa, where the

Denhams had spent a week; I turned the conversation on the church of St. Lorenzo and the relic in the treasury there—the Sacra Catino, a supposed gift to Solomon from the Queen of Sheba. Miss Denham listened with the calmest interest; she had not seen it the day she visited the church; she was sorry to have missed that. Then the aunt changed the subject, but whether by accident or design I was unable for the soul of me to conjecture. Good God, Flemming! could this girl have had some terrible, swift malady which touched her and passed, and still hangs over her—an hereditary doom?"

"Then she's the most artful actress that ever lived, I should say. The leading lady of the Theatre Francais might go and take lessons of her. But if that were so, Ned?"

"If that were so," said Lynde slowly, "a great pity would be added to my love."

"You would not marry her!"

Lynde made no reply.

The night had settled down upon Geneva while the friends were talking. The room was so dark they could not distinguish each other; but Flemming was conscious of a pale, set face turned towards him in the obscurity, in the same way that he was conscious of the forlorn whiteness of Mont Blanc looming up out yonder, unseen. It was dark in the chamber, but the streets were gay now with the life of a midsummer night. Interminable lines of lamps twinkled on the bridges and along the quays; the windows of the cafes on the opposite bank of the Rhone were brilliant with gas jets; boats, bearing merry cargoes to and from the lake, passed up and down the river; the street running under the hotel balcony was crowded with loungers, and a band was playing in the English Garden. From time to time a strain of music floated up to the window where the two men were sitting. Neither had spoken for some minutes, when Lynde asked his friend where he was staying.

"At the Schweizerhof," replied Flemming. "I always take the hotel nearest the station. Few Americans go there, I fancy. It is wonderfully and fearfully Swiss. I was strolling in here to look through the register for some American autographs when I ran against you."

"You had better bring your traps over here."

"It would not be worth while. I am booked for Paris to-morrow night. Ned—come with me!"

"I can't, Flemming; I have agreed to go to Chamouni with the Denhams."

"Don't!"

"That is like advising a famishing man not to eat his last morsel of food. I have a presentiment it will all end there. I never had a presentiment before."

"I had a presentiment once," said Flemming impressively. "I had a presentiment that a certain number—it was number twenty-seven—would draw the prize in a certain lottery. I went to the office, and number twenty-seven was one of the two numbers unsold! I bought it as quick as lightning, I dreamed of number twenty-seven three successive nights, and the next day it drew a blank."

"That has the ring of the old Flemming!" cried Lynde, with an unforced laugh. "I am glad that I have not succeeded in turning all your joyous gold into lead. I'm not always such dull company as I have been to-night, with my moods and my presentiments. I owe them partly, perhaps, to not seeing Miss Denham to-day, the aunt having a headache."

"You were not in a rollicking humor when I picked you up."

"I had been cruising about town all the morning alone, making assaults on the Musee Fol, the Botanic Garden, and the Jewish Synagogue. In the afternoon I had wrecked myself on Rousseau's Island, where I sat on a bench staring at Pradier's poor statue of Jean Jacques until I fancied that the ugly bronze cannibal was making mouths at me. When the aunt has a headache, *I* suffer. Flemming, you must see Miss Denham, if only for a moment."

"Of course I should like to see her, Ned."

"You do not leave until evening," Lynde said, reflecting. "I think I can manage a little dinner for to-morrow. Now let us take a breath of fresh air. I know the queerest old nook, in the Rue de Chantpoulet, where the Bavarian beer is excellent and all the company smoke the most enormous porcelain pipes. Haven't I hit one of your weaknesses?"

"You have hit a brace!"

VII

THE DENHAMS

When Edward Lynde returned to the hotel that night, after parting with Flemming at the head of a crooked, gable-hung street leading to the Schweizerhof, the young man regretted that he had said anything on the subject of the Denhams, or rather, that he had spoken of the painful likeness which had haunted him so persistently. The friends had spent the gayest of evenings together at a small green-topped table in one corner of the smoky cafe. Over their beer and cheese they had chatted of old days at boarding-school and college, and this contact with the large, healthy nature of Flemming, which threw off depression as sunshine dissipates mist, had sent Lynde's vapors flying. Nothing was changed in the circumstances that had distressed him, yet some way a load had removed itself from his bosom. He was sorry he had mentioned that dark business at all. As he threaded the deserted streets—it was long after midnight—he planned a dinner to be given in his rooms the next day, and formulated a note of invitation to the ladies, which he would write when he got back to the hotel, and have in readiness for early delivery in the morning.

Lynde was in one of those lightsome moods which, in that varying month, had not unfrequently followed a day of doubt and restless despondency. As he turned into the Quai des Bergues he actually hummed a bar or two of opera. He had not done that before in six weeks. They had been weeks of inconceivable torment and pleasure to Lynde.

He had left home while still afflicted by David Lynde's death. Since the uncle's ill-advised marriage the intercourse between them, as the reader knows, had all but ceased; they had met only once, and then as if to bid each other farewell; but the ties had been very close, after all. In the weeks immediately following his guardian's death, the young man, occupied with settling the estate, of which he was one of the executors, scarcely realized his loss; but when he returned to Rivermouth a heavy sense of loneliness came over him. The crowded, happy firesides to which he was free seemed to reproach him for his lack of kinship; he stood alone in the world; there was no more reason why he should stay in one place than in another. His connection with the bank, unnecessary now from a money point of view, grew irksome; the quietude of the town oppressed him; he determined to cut adrift from all and go abroad. An educated American with no deeper sorrow than Lynde's cannot travel through Europe, for the first time at least, with indifference. Three months in Germany and France began in Lynde a cure which was completed by a winter in Southern Italy. He had regained his former elasticity of spirits and was taking life with a relish, when he went to Geneva; there he fell in with the Denhams in the manner he described to Flemming. An habitual shyness, and perhaps a doubt of Flemming's sympathetic capacity, had prevented Lynde from giving his friend more than an outline of the situation. In his statement Lynde had omitted several matters which may properly be set down here.

That first day at the table d'hote and the next day, when he was able more deliberately to study the young woman, Edward Lynde had made no question to himself as to her being the same person he had seen in so different and so pathetic surroundings. It was unmistakably the same. He had even had a vague apprehension she might recognize him, and had been greatly relieved to observe that there was no glimmer of recognition in the well-bred, careless glance which swept him once or twice. No, he had passed out of her memory— with the other shapes and shadows! How strange they should meet again, thousands of miles from New England; how strange that he alone, of all the crowded city, should know there had been a dark episode in this girl's history! What words she had spoken to him and forgotten, she who now sat there robed in the beauty of her reason!

It was a natural interest, and a deep interest, certainly, that impelled Lynde to seek the acquaintance of the two ladies. On the third day a chance service rendered the elder—she had left a glove or a handkerchief beside her plate at table, and Lynde had followed her with it from the dining-room—placed him upon speaking terms. They were his country-women, he was a gentleman, and the surface ice was easily broken. Three days afterwards Lynde found himself oddly doubting his first conviction. This was not that girl! The likeness was undeniable: the same purple-black hair, the same long eyelashes, a very distinctive feature. In voice and carriage, too, Miss Denham curiously recalled the other; and that mark on Miss Denham's cheek—a birth-mark—was singular enough. But there the analogies ended. Miss Denham was a young woman who obviously had seen much of the world; she possessed accomplishments which could have been acquired only by uninterrupted application; she spoke French, German, and Italian with unusual purity. That intellect, as strong and clear as crystal, could never have suffered even a temporary blur. He was beginning to be amazed at the blunder he had committed, when suddenly, one evening, a peculiar note in her voice, accompanied by a certain lifting of the eyelashes—a movement he had noticed for the first time, but which was familiar to him—threw Lynde into great perplexity. It WAS that other girl! How useless for him to try to blind himself to the truth! Besides, why should he wish to, and why should the fact of the identity trouble him to such a degree? The next day he was staggered by Miss Denham alluding incidentally to the circumstance that she and her aunt had passed a part of the spring of 1872 in Florida. That was the date of Lynde's adventure, the spring of 1872. Here was almost positive proof that Miss Denham could not have been in New England at the time. Lynde did not know what to think. Of course he was mistaken; he must be mistaken—and yet! There were moments when he could not look at Miss Denham without half expecting to see the man Blaisdell flitting somewhere in the background. Then there were days when it was impossible for Lynde to picture her as anything different from what she now was. But whatever conclusion he came to, a doubt directly insinuated itself.

While he was drifting from one uncertainty to another, a fortnight elapsed in which his intimacy with the Denhams had daily increased. They were in Geneva for an indefinite time, awaiting directions from Mr. Denham. The few sights in the city had been exhausted; the places of interest in the environs could not be visited by ladies without escort; so it fell out that Lynde accompanied the Denhams on several short excursions—to Petit and Grand Sacconnex, to the Villa Tronchin, to Pregny and Mornex. These were days which Lynde marked with a red letter. At the end of the month, however, he was in the same state of distressing indecision relative to Miss Denham. On one point he required no light—he was deeply interested in her, so deeply, indeed, that it had become a question affecting all his future, whether or not she was the person he had encountered on his horseback journey three years before. If she was—

But Edward Lynde had put the question out of his thought that night as he walked home from the cafe. His two bars of opera music lasted him to the hotel steps. Though it was late—a great bell somewhere, striking two, sent its rich reverberation across the lake while he was unlocking his chamber door— Lynde seated himself at a table and wrote his note to the Denhams.

Flemming had promised to come and take coffee with him early the next morning, that is to say at nine o'clock. Before Flemming arrived, Lynde's invitation had been despatched and accepted. He was re-reading Miss Denham's few lines of acceptance when he heard his friend, at the other end of the hall, approaching with great strides.

"The thousandth part of a minute late!" cried Flemming, throwing open the door. "There's no excuse for me. When a man lives in a city where they manufacture a hundred thousand watches a year—that's one watch and a quarter every five minutes day and night—it's a moral duty to be punctual. Ned, you look like a prize pink this morning."

"I have had such a sleep! Besides, I've just gone through the excitement of laying out the menu for our dinner. Good heavens, I forgot the flowers! We'll go and get them after breakfast. There's your coffee. Cream, old man? I am in a tremor over this dinner, you know. It is a maiden effort. By the way, Flemming, I wish you'd forget what I said about Miss Denham, last evening. I was all wrong."

"I told you so; what has happened?"

"Nothing. Only I have reconsidered the matter, and I see I was wrong to let it upset me."

"I saw that from the first."

"Some persons," said Lynde gayly, "always see everything from the first. You belong to the I-told-you-so family, only you belong to the cheerful branch."

"Thank the Lord for that! A wide-spreading, hopeful disposition is your only true umbrella in this vale of tears."

"I shall have to borrow yours, then, if it rains heavily, for I've none of my own."

"Take it, my boy; my name's on the handle!"

On finishing their coffee the young men lighted cigars and sallied forth for a stroll along the bank of the river, which they followed to the confluence of the Rhone with the Arve, stopping on the way to leave an order at a florist's. Returning to the hotel some time after mid-day, they found the flowers awaiting them in Lynde's parlor, where a servant was already laying the cloth. There were bouquets for the ladies' plates, an imposing centre-piece in the shape of a pyramid, and a profusion of loose flowers.

"What shall we do with these?" asked Lynde, pointing to the latter.

"Set 'em around somewhere," said Flemming, with cheerful vagueness.

Lynde disposed the flowers around the room to the best of his judgment; he hung some among the glass pendants of the chandelier, gave a nosegay to each of the two gilt statuettes in the corners, and piled the remainder about the base of a monumental clock on the mantelpiece.

"That's rather a pretty idea, isn't it?—wreathing Time in flowers," remarked Flemming, with honest envy of his friend's profounder depth of poetic sentiment.

"I thought it rather neat," said Lynde, who had not thought of it at all.

In the course of that dinner if two or three unexplained demure smiles flitted over Miss Denham's face, they might, perhaps, have been indirectly traced to these floral decorations, though they pleased her more than if a woman's hand had been visible in them.

"Flemming," said Lynde, with a severe aesthetic air, "I don't think that arrangement in the fireplace is quite up to the rest of the room."

"Nor I either," said Flemming, who had been silently admiring it for the last ten minutes.

The fireplace in question was stuffed with a quantity of long, delicately spiral shavings, sprinkled with silver spangles or flakes of isinglass, and covered by a piece of pale blue illusion. This device—peculiarly Genevese—was supposed to represent a waterfall.

"Take a match and touch it off," suggested Flemming.

"If we had some more flowers, now"—"Exactly. I am going to the hotel to get myself up like a head-waiter, and I'll bring some when I come back."

In an hour afterwards Flemming reappeared, followed by a youth bearing an immense basket. Lynde removed the Alpine waterfall to an adjoining chamber, and built up a huge fire of flame-colored flowers in the grate. The two friends were standing in the middle of the room, gravely contemplating the effect, when a servant opened the door and announced Mrs. and Miss Denham. A rustle of drapery at the threshold was followed by the entrance of the two ladies in ceremonious dinner toilets.

Lynde had never seen Miss Denham in any but a dark travelling-dress, or in such unobtrusive costume as a modest girl may wear at a hotel table. He stood motionless an instant, seeing her in a trailing robe of some fleecy, maize-colored material, with a cluster of moss-roses at her corsage and a cross of diamonds at her throat. She was without other ornament. The shade of her dress made her hair and eyes and complexion wonderful. Lynde was proud to have her look like that for Flemming, though he was himself affected by a queer impression that this queenly young person was not the simple, lovely girl he had known all along. He was embarrassed by her unexpected elegance, but he covered his embarrassment and his pleasure by presenting his friend to the ladies, and ordering the servant to serve the dinner immediately.

Lynde's constraint was only momentary, and the others had experienced none. Flemming, indeed, had a fleeting surprise at finding in the aunt a woman of thirty-five or thirty-eight, in the Indian summer of her beauty. Lynde had given him the idea of an elderly person with spectacles. As to Miss Denham, she had not fallen short of the mental picture Flemming had drawn of her—which ought to have surprised him. No charms or graces in a woman, however, could much surprise Flemming; he accepted them as matters of course; to him all women were charming in various degrees. He had that general susceptibility which preserves us the breed of bachelors. The constant victim of a series of minor emotions, he was safe from any major passion. There was a certain chivalrous air of camaraderie in his manner to women which made them like him sooner or later; the Denhams liked him instantly. Even before the potage was removed, Lynde saw that his dinner was a success. "The cook may drop dead now, if he wants to," said Lynde to himself; "he can't spoil anything."

"You are not entirely a stranger to us, Mr. Flemming," said Mrs. Denham, looking at him from behind the floral pyramid, which had the happy effect of isolating two guests who sat opposite each other. "There is a person who goes about foreign lands with no other ostensible mission than to sound your praise."

"You must set down a great deal to filial gratitude," returned Flemming. "I have been almost a father to our young friend."

"He tells me that your being here is quite accidental."

"It was one of those fortunate things, madam, which sometimes befall undeserving persons, as if to refute the theory of a special providence."

"On the contrary, Mr. Flemming"—it was Miss Ruth who spoke—"it was evidently arranged with the clearest foresight; for if you had been a day later, perhaps you would not have found your friend in Geneva—that is, if Mr. Lynde goes with us to Chamouni."

"You have heard from Mr. Denham, then?" said Lynde, turning to the aunt.

"We had letters this morning. Mr. Denham is in Paris, where he will remain a week or ten days, to show the sights to an old American friend of ours who is to join our party. I think I told you, Mr. Lynde? Supposing us to be weary of Geneva by this time, Mr. Denham suggests that we go on to Chamouni and wait there. I have left the matter to Ruth, and she decides in favor of leaving to-morrow, if the weather is fine."

"We are not tired of Geneva," said Miss Denham; "it would be ingratitude to Mr. Lynde to admit that; but we are longing for a nearer view of the Mont Blanc groups. One ought to know them pretty well after six weeks' constant looking at them; but the changes in the atmosphere make any certain intimacy impossible at this distance. New ranges loom up and disappear, the lines alter almost every hour. Were you ever at the Isles of Shoals, Mr. Flemming?"

Flemming started slightly. Since Miss Denham entered the room, he had given scarcely a thought to Lynde's dismal suspicions. Once or twice they had come into Flemming's mind, but he had promptly dismissed them. The girl's inquiry concerning a locality in New Hampshire suddenly recalled them, and recalled the motive with which Lynde had planned the dinner. Flemming flushed with vexation to think he had lent himself to the arrangement.

"I have spent parts of two summers at the Isles of Shoals," he said.

"Then you must have observed the singular changes that seem to take place on the mainland, seen from Appledore. The mirage on the Rye and Newcastle coasts—is it Newcastle?—sometimes does wonderful things. Frequently you see great cities stretching along the beach, some of the houses rising out of the water, as in Venice, only they are gloomy, foggy cities, like London, and not like Venice. Another time you see ships sailing by upside down; then it is a chain of hills, with peaks and projections that melt away under your eyes, leaving only the flat coast-line."

Flemming had seen all this, and seemed again to see it through the clear medium of the young girl's words. He had witnessed similar optical illusions in the deserts, also, which he described to her. Then he remembered a curious trick of refracted light he had once seen in the sunrise on Mount Washington, and suddenly he found himself asking Miss Denham if she were acquainted with the interior of New Hampshire. Flemming had put the interrogation without a shadow of design; he could have bitten his tongue off an instant after.

Lynde, who had been discussing with Mrs. Denham the details of the next day's journey, looked up quickly and sent Flemming a rapid scowl.

"I have never been inland," was Miss Denham's answer. "My acquaintance with New Hampshire is limited to the Shoals and the beaches at Rye and

Hampton. In visiting the Alps first I have, I know, been very impolite to the mountains and hills of my own land."

"Ruth, dear, Mr. Lynde and I have been speaking of the conveyance for to-morrow; shall it be an open or a close carriage?"

"An open carriage, by all means, aunt."

"That would have its inconvenience in case of showers," said Lynde; "when April takes her departure from the Alps, she is said to leave all her capriciousness behind her. I suggest a partially closed vehicle; you will find a covering comfortable in either rain or shine."

"Mr. Lynde thinks of everything," remarked Mrs. Denham. "He should not allow himself to be dictated to by unforeseeing woman."

"In strict confidence, Mrs. Denham, I will confess that I have arbitrarily taken this business in hand. For nearly a week, now, I have had my eye on a vehicle that must have been built expressly for us; it is driven by a tall, distinguished person, frosty of mustache and affable of manner—evidently a French marquis in disguise."

"What an adroit fellow Ned is!" Flemming said to himself. "I wonder that with all his cleverness he could have got such a foolish notion into his head about this girl."

"We must have the French marquis at any cost," said Miss Denham.

"The truth is," remarked Lynde, "I have secured him."

"We are to start at eight, Ruth."

"Which means breakfast at seven. Is Mr. Lynde equal to a feat like that, aunt?"

"As I intend to have watchers and sit up all night," said Lynde, "I think I can promise to be on hand."

This matter decided, the conversation, which had been carried on mostly in duets, became general. Flemming soon recovered from the remorse of his inadvertent question, or rather from his annoyance at the thought that possibly it had struck Lynde as having an ulterior motive.

As to Lynde, he was in the highest humor. Miss Denham had been thoroughly charming to his friend, with her serious and candid manner—a manner as far removed from reserve as from the thin vivacity of the average young woman of the period. Her rare smile had been finer than another's laugh. Flemming himself went as near to falling in love with her and the aunt as his loyalty to Lynde and the supposed existence of a Mr. Denham permitted.

After a while the window curtains were drawn, though it was scarcely dusk without, and candles brought; then the ices were served, and then the coffee;

and then the clock on the mantelpiece, as if it took malicious satisfaction in the fleetness with which Time (wreathed in flowers) slips away from mortals, set up a silvery chime—it sounded like the angelus rung from some cathedral in the distance—to tell Flemming that his hour was come. He had still to return to the hotel to change his dress-suit before taking the train. Mrs. Denham insisted on Lynde accompanying his friend to the station, though Flemming had begged that he might be allowed to withdraw without disturbing the party, and even without saying farewell. "I don't recognize good-bys," said he; "there are too many sorrowful partings in the world already. I never give them the slightest encouragement." But the ladies persisted in considering the dinner at an end; then the two friends conducted the Denhams to the door of their own parlor and there took leave of them.

"Well?" said Lynde as he seated himself beside Flemming in the carriage. "What do you think of her?"

"An unusually agreeable woman," returned Flemming carelessly. "She is thirty-eight, she looks twenty-six, and is as pleasant as nineteen."

"I mean Miss Denham!"

"Ned, I don't care to discuss Miss Denham. When I think of your connecting that lovely lady with a crazy creature you met somewhere or other, I am troubled touching your intellect."

"But I do not any longer connect her with that unfortunate girl. I told you to put all that out of your mind."

"I don't find it easy to do, Ned; it is so monstrous. Was not this dinner an arrangement for me to see Miss Denham and in some way judge her?"

"No, Flemming; there was a moment yesterday evening when I had some such wild idea. I had grown morbid by being alone all day and brooding over a resemblance which I have not been able to prevent affecting me disagreeably at intervals. This resemblance does not exist for you, and you have not been subtle enough to put yourself in my place. However, all that is past; it shall not disturb me in future. When I invited the Denhams to this dinner it was solely that I might present you to the woman I shall marry if she will have me."

"She is too good for you, Ned."

"I know it. That's one thing makes me love her. I admire superior people; it is my single merit. I wouldn't stoop to marry my equal. Flemming, what possessed you to question her about New Hampshire?"

"We were speaking of the White Hills, and the question asked itself. I wasn't thinking of your puerilities; don't imagine it. I hope her reply settled you. What are you going to do now?"

"I shall go with them to Chamouni."

"And afterwards?"

"My plan is to wait there until the uncle comes."

"That would be an excellent plan if you wanted to marry the uncle. If I were you, Ned, I would go and speak with Miss Denham, and then with the aunt, who will be worth a dozen uncles if you enlist her on your side. She doesn't seem unfriendly to you."

"I will do that, Flemming," returned Lynde thoughtfully. "I am not sure that Miss Denham would marry me. We are disposing of her as if she could be had for the asking. I might lose everything by being premature."

"Premature! I've a mind to stay over and fall in love with her myself. I could do it in a day and a half, and you have been six weeks about it."

"Six weeks! I sometimes think I have loved her all my life," said Lynde.

From the Schweizerhof the young men drove without speaking to the railroad station, which they reached just in time for Flemming to catch his train. With hurriedly exchanged promises to write each other, the two parted on the platform. Then Lynde in a serenely happy frame of mind caused himself to be driven to the Rue des Paquis, where he stopped at the chateau of the French marquis, which looked remarkably like a livery-stable, and arranged for a certain travelling-carriage to be at the door of the hotel the next morning at eight.

VIII

FROM GENEVA TO CHAMOUNI

If there is in all the world as lovely a day's ride as that from Geneva to Chamouni, it must be the ride from Chamouni to Geneva. Lynde would not have made even this concession the next morning, as a heavy-wheeled carriage, containing three travellers and drawn by four stout Savoy horses, rolled through the Grande Place, and, amid a salvo of whip-lash and a cloud of dust, took the road to Bonneville.

"I did not think I cared very much for Geneva," said Miss Denham, leaning from the carriage side to look back at the little Swiss capital set so prettily on the blue edge of Lake Leman; "I did not think I cared for it at all; yet I leave it with a kind of home-leaving regret."

"That is because you found complete repose there, I imagine," said Lynde. "Geneva is blessed among foreign cities in having no rich picture-galleries, or famous cathedrals, or mouldy ruins covered all over with moss and history. In other places, you know, one is distracted by the things which it is one's imperative duty to see, and by the feeling that a lifetime is too short properly to see them. Coming from the great Italian cities to Geneva is like falling asleep after some prolonged mental strain. I do not object to waking up and leaving it, however. I should not mind leaving Eden, in pleasant company, on such a morning as this."

"The company, and I dare say the morning, are not insensible to your handsome compliment, Mr. Lynde."

The morning was without flaw, and the company, or at least that part of it represented by Miss Ruth Denham, had more color in its cheeks than usual, and its dark eyes looked very dark and melting under their long fringes. Mrs. Denham was also of a high complexion, but, having a practical turn of mind, she was wondering whether the trunks, which rose like a monument from the footboard of the vehicle, were quite secure. It was a lumbering, comfortable concern, with red and black wheels, and a maroon body set upon complicated springs. The back seat, occupied by the Denhams, was protected by a leather hood, leaving the forward portion of the carriage open. The other seat was amicably shared between Lynde and a pile of waterproofs and woollen wraps, essentials in Switzerland, but which the ladies doubtless would have provided themselves if they had been in the tropics. On the high box in front sat the driver, speaking from time to time in low, confidential tones to the four powerful black horses, whose harnesses were lavishly hung with flaunting chamois-tails and made merry with innumerable silver bells.

For the last two weeks Lynde had been impatiently looking forward to this journey. The thought of having an entire day with Miss Denham, on such terms of intimacy as tacitly establish themselves between persons travelling together in the same carriage, had softened the prospect of the final parting at Chamouni; though now he did not intend they should separate there, unless she cruelly willed it. The nature of Miss Denham's regard for him Lynde had not fathomed. She had been frank and friendly with him, as she might have been with a cousin or a person much older than herself. As he told Flemming, he had never had her a minute alone. The aunt had always accompanied them on their brief walks and excursions about Geneva; whenever she had been unable to do so, the excursion or the walk had been abandoned. Lynde saw, among other gracious things in this day's ride, a promising opportunity for a tete-a-tete with Miss Denham. Here and there, along the winding ascents, would be tempting foot-paths, short pine—shaded cuts across the rocks, by which the carriage could be intercepted farther on. These five or ten minutes' walks, always made enchanting by some unlooked-for grove, or grotto, or cascade, were nearly certain to lure Miss Ruth to her feet. Then he would have her to himself, for Mrs. Denham seldom walked when she could avoid it. To make assurance doubly sure Lynde could almost have wished her one of those distracting headaches from which hitherto he had suffered so keenly.

For the first few miles the road lay through a succession of villas and cultivated gardens; indeed, these gardens and villas extend all the way to Chene, where a thin ribbon of a stream, the Foron, draws the boundary line between the canton of Geneva and Savoy. At this point the scenery begins, not too aggressively, to be picturesque; you catch some neat views of the Voirons, and of the range of the Jura lying on your right. Beyond is the village of Annemasse, and the Chateau of Etrambiere, with its quartette of towers, rises from the foot of the Petit-Saleve in the bluish-gray distance. You no longer see Mont Blanc, except at intervals. Here and there a knot of hamlets clings to some fir-dotted slope, or tries to hide itself away in the bosom of a ravine. All these Alpine villages bear the same resemblance to one another as so many button-moulds of different sizes. Each has its quaint little church of stucco, surrounded by clusters of gray and dingy-white head-stones and crosses—like a shepherd standing in the midst of his flock; each has its bedrabbled main street, with a great stone trough into which a stream of ice-cold water is forever flowing, and where comely young women of substantial ankles, with their flaxen hair braided down their backs, are forever washing linen; each has its beggar, with a goitre or a wooden leg, lying in wait for you; and each, in turn, with its purple and green and red tiled roofs, is charming to approach and delightful to get away from.

After leaving Annemasse, the road runs up the valley of the Arve and crosses a bridge over the Menoge. Then comes the village of Nangy, and then Contamines, beyond which, on a bold height, stand the two wrinkled, crumbling towers of the ancient castle of Faucigny, whence the province takes its name. It was at Nangy that a pretty incident befell our travellers. On the outskirts of the village they met fifty or sixty school-children marching three abreast, the girls on one side of the road and the boys on the other. The girls—each in a coarse blue or yellow frock, with a snowy neckerchief pinned over her bosom and a pig-tail of hair hanging down her shoulders—seemed for all the world like little old women; and not one of the little men appeared to be less than a hundred and five years old. They suggested a collection of Shems and Japhets, with their wives, taken from a lot of toy Noah's arks. As the carriage rolled between the two files, all the funny little women bobbed a simultaneous courtesy, and all the little old-fashioned men lifted their hats with the most irresistible gravity conceivable. "Fancy such a thing happening in the United States!" said Lynde. "If we were to meet such a crowd at home, half a dozen urchins would immediately fasten themselves to the hind axle, and some of the more playful spirits would probably favor us with a stone or two, or a snowball, according to the season."

"There comes the curee, now," said Miss Denham. "It is some Sunday-school fete."

As the curee, a florid, stout person, made an obeisance and passed on, fanning himself leisurely with his shovel-hat, his simple round face and white feathery hair put Lynde in mind of the hapless old gentleman whom he mistook for the country parson that morning so long ago. Instantly the whole scene rose before Lynde's vision. Perhaps the character of the landscape through which they were passing helped to make the recollection very vivid. There was not a cloud in the pale arch; yonder were the far-reaching peaks with patches of snow on them, and there stretched the same rugged, forlorn hills, covered with dwarf bushes and sentinelled with phantom-like pines. An odd expression drifted across Lynde's countenance.

"What are you smiling at, Mr. Lynde, in that supremely selfish manner?" inquired Mrs. Denham, looking at him from under her tilted sun-umbrella.

"Was I smiling? It was at those droll little beggars. They bowed and courtesied in an unconcerned, wooden way, as if they were moved by some ingenious piece of Swiss clock-work. The stiff old curee, too, had an air of having been wound up and set a-going. I could almost hear the creak of his mainspring. I was smiling at that, perhaps, and thinking how strongly the scenery of some portions of our own country resembles this part of Switzerland."

"Do you think so? I had not remarked it."

"This is not the least like anything in the Adirondack region, for example," observed Miss Ruth.

"It may be a mere fancy of mine," returned Lynde. "However, we have similar geological formations in the mountainous sections of New England; the same uncompromising Gothic sort of pines; the same wintry bleakness that leaves its impress even on the midsummer. A body of water tumbling through a gorge in New Hampshire must be much like a body of water tumbling through a gorge anywhere else."

"Undoubtedly all mountain scenery has many features in common," Mrs. Denham said; "but if I were dropped down on the White Hills, softly from a balloon, let us say, I should know in a second I was not in Switzerland."

"I should like to put you to the test in one spot I am familiar with," said Lynde.

"I should not like to be put to the test just at present," rejoined Mrs. Denham. "I am very simple in my tastes, and I prefer the Alps."

"Where in New England will you see such a picture as that?" asked Miss Ruth, pointing to a village which lay in the heart of the valley, shut in on the right by the jagged limestone rocks of the Brezon and on the left by the grassy slopes of the Mole.

"Our rural towns lack color and architecture," said Lynde. "They are mostly collections of square or oblong boxes, painted white. I wish we had just one village composed exclusively of rosy-tiled houses, with staircases wantonly running up on the outside, and hooded windows, and airy balconies hanging out here and there where you don't expect them. I would almost overlook the total lack of drainage which seems to go along with these carved eaves and gables, touched in with their blues and browns and yellows. This must be Bonnevine we are coming to. We change horses here."

In a few minutes they swept through an avenue of noble trees, and stopped at the doorstep of an inn alive with passengers by the diligence just arrived from Sallanches, on its way to Geneva.

Lynde was beginning to feel a trifle out of spirits. The journey thus far had been very pleasant, but it had not wholly fulfilled his expectations. The Denhams had occupied themselves with the scenery; they had not been much inclined to talk; and Lynde had; found no opportunity to make himself especially agreeable. They had spoken several times of Flemming, in a vein of eulogy. Lynde loved Flemming; but Flemming as a topic of conversation possessed no particular advantage over landscape. Miss Denham had never looked so lovely to Lynde as she did this day; he was glad to get her again in that closely fitting drab travelling-dress, laced up to the shapely white throat. A sense of great comfort had stolen over him the two or three times when she had sunk back in the carriage cushions and let her eyes dwell upon him contemplatively for a moment. He was beginning to hate Mrs. Denham, and he thoroughly loathed Bonneville, where a polyglot crowd of tourists came flocking into the small waiting-room just as Miss Ruth was putting up her hair and unconsciously framing for Lynde a never-to-be-forgotten picture in the little cracked inn-mirror.

Passengers by diligence usually dine at Bonneville, a fact which Lynde had ascertained when he selected Cluses, nine miles beyond, as the resting-place for his own party. They were soon on the road again, with the black horses turned into roan, traversing the level meadow lands between the Brezon and the Mole. With each mile, now, the landscape took on new beauty and wildness. The superb mountains—some with cloudy white turrets, some thrusting out huge snow-powdered prongs, and others tapering to steely dagger-points—hemmed them in on every side.

Here they came more frequently on those sorrowful roadside cairns, surmounted by a wooden cross with an obliterated inscription and a shrivelled wreath, marking the spot where some peasant or mountaineer had been crushed by a land-slide or smothered in the merciless winter drift. As the carriage approached Cluses, the road crept along the lips of precipices and was literally overhung by the dizzy walls of the Brezon. Crossing the Arve—you are always crossing the Arve or some mad torrent on your way from Geneva to Chamouni—the travellers entered the town of Cluses and alighted at one of those small Swiss hotels which continually astonish by their tidiness and excellence.

In spite of the intermittent breeze wandering down from the regions above the snow-line, the latter part of the ride had been intensely hot. The cool, shadowy room, with its table ready laid for dinner near the latticed window, was a welcome change to the three dusty voyagers as they were ushered into it by the German landlord, whose round head thinly thatched with whitey-brown hair gave him the appearance of having been left out over night in a hoar frost. It was a refreshment in itself to look at him, so crisp and cool, with that blinding afternoon glare lying on the heated mountain-slopes.

"I could be contented here a month," said Mrs. Denham, throwing off her bonnet, and seating herself in the embrasure of the window.

"The marquis allows us only three quarters of an hour," Lynde observed. "He says we cannot afford to lose much time if we want to reach Chamouni before sundown."

"Chamouni will wait for us."

"But the sunset won't."

Lynde had a better reason than that for wishing to press on. It was between there and Magland, or, rather, just beyond Magland, that he proposed to invite Miss Denham to walk. The wonderful cascade of Arpenaz, though it could be seen as well from the carriage, was to serve as pretext. Of course he would be obliged to include Mrs. Denham in his invitation, and he had sufficient faith in the inconsistency of woman not to rely too confidently on her declining. "As she never walks, she'll come along fast enough," was Lynde's grim reflection.

He had by no means resolved on what he should say to Miss Ruth, if he got her alone. In the ten minutes' walk, which would be almost equivalent to a first interview, he could not say much. He could tell her how grieved he was at the thought of the approaching separation, and tell her in such a manner as would leave her in no great doubt as to the state of his feelings. But whether he went so far as that was a problem which he intended to let chance solve for him.

Lynde was standing on the inn steps with his after-dinner cheroot, meditatively blowing circles of smoke into the air, when the carriage drove round from the stable and the Denhams appeared in the doorway. The young woman gave Lynde an ungloved hand as he assisted her to the seat. The slight pressure of her fingers and the touch of her rings were possessions which he retained until long after the carriage had passed that narrow defile near the stalactite cavern in the Balme, where a couple of tiresome fellows insist on letting off a small cannon for you, to awaken a very disobliging old Echo who refuses to repeat anything more than twice. What a magic there is in hands— in some hands! Lynde could have held Mrs. Denham's hand a fortnight without getting anything so tangible as that fleeting touch of Miss Ruth's.

"Is the grotto worth seeing?" Mrs. Denham asked, with a speculative glance up the mountain side.

"It is an hour's hard climb, and scarcely pays," replied Lynde, appalled by this indication of Alpine enterprise. "I visited it the first time I came over the road. You get a good look at the peaks of Mont Douron on the other side of the valley, and that's all; the grotto itself is not remarkable. But I think it will be worth while to halt a moment when we come to the fall of Nant d'Arpenaz. That is really marvellous. It is said to be nearly as fine as the Staubbach."

As Miss Ruth leaned back in the cushions, lazily fastening the third button of her glove with a hair-pin, there was just the faintest glimmer of humor in the eyes that looked up into the young man's face. He was being read, and he knew it; his dark intentions in regard to that waterfall were probably as legible to her as if they had been printed in great-primer type on his forehead. On two or three occasions at Geneva she had wrested his unworded thought from him with the same effortless sorcery. Lynde evaded her look, and studied a spire-like peak on his left. "I shall have an air of detected villainy now, when I ask her," he mused. "That's the first shade of coquetry I ever saw in her. If she accepts my invitation without the aunt, she means either to flirt with me or give me the chance to speak to her seriously. Which is it to be, Miss Ruth? I wonder if she is afraid of Mrs. Denham. Sometimes it seems to me she would be a different girl if it were not for the presence of the aunt."

By and by, at a bend of the road after passing Magland, the waterfall became visible in the distance. The cascade of Nant d'Arpenaz is one of the highest falls in Savoy, and if it is not the most beautiful, one can still well afford, having seen that, not to see the others. It is not a large volume of water, except when swollen by rains, as it happened to be this day, but its plunge from the dizzy brown cliff is the gracefulest thing in the world. The curiously stratified face of the precipice is concave, and the water has a fall of several hundred feet to reach the slope, which, indeed, it seems never to reach; for before the stream has accomplished half the descent it is broken into fine spray, and flaunts loosely in the wind like a veil of the most delicate lace, or, when the sunlight drifts through it, a wondrously wrought Persian scarf. There it appears to hang, miraculously suspended in mid-air, while in fact it descends in imperceptible vapors to the slope, where it re-forms and becomes a furious little torrent that dashes across the road under a bridge and empties itself into the Arve.

The carriage-road skirts the base of the mountain and offers numberless fine views of the cascade as you approach or leave it. It was directly in front of the fall, half a mile distant, though it did not look so far, that the driver, in obedience to previous instruction from Lynde, drew up the horses and halted. At that instant the sunshine slanted across the fall and dashed it with prismatic colors.

"It is almost too exquisite to look at," said Mrs. Denham. "It makes one doubt one's own eyes."

"I saw it once," Lynde said, "when I thought the effect even finer. I was induced by some pleasant English tourists to stop over night at Magland, and we walked up here in the moonrise. You can't imagine anything so lovely as that long strip of gossamer unfolding itself to the moonlight. There was an English artist with us, who made a sketch of the fall; but he said a prettier thing about it than his picture."

"What was that?" inquired Miss Ruth.

"He called it Penelope's web, because it is always being unravelled and reknitted."

"That artist mistook his profession."

"Folks often do," said Lynde. "I know painters who ought to be poets, and poets who ought to be bricklayers."

"Why bricklayers?"

"Because I fancy that bricklaying makes as slight drain on the imagination as almost any pursuit in life. Speaking of poets and waterfalls, do you remember Byron's daring simile in Manfred? He compares a certain waterfall at the foot of the Jungfrau to the tail of the pale horse ridden by Death in the Apocalypse. Mrs. Denham," said Lynde abruptly, "the marquis tells me there's a delightful short cut, through the rocks here, which strikes into the road a mile further on."

"Let us take it then," answered Mrs. Denham, settling herself comfortably in the cushions.

"It is a foot-path," explained Lynde.

"Oh!"

"Our reputation as great American travellers will suffer, Mrs. Denham, if we fail to do a bit of Switzerland on foot. Rather than have that happen I would undertake the expedition alone. It would be mere martyrdom, though, without company." As Lynde turned the handle of the carriage door and planted his foot on the first step, he ventured a glance at Miss Ruth, who was sitting there with a face as impenetrable as that of the Memphian Sphinx.

"Certainly, if our reputation is at stake," exclaimed Mrs. Denham, rising with alacrity. Lynde could not help his clouded countenance. "No," she added, slowly sinking back into the seat, "I've no ambition as an explorer. I really have not."

"And Miss Denham?" said Lynde, drawing a scarcely repressed breath of relief.

"Oh, Ruth can go if she likes," replied Mrs. Denham, "provided it is not too far."

"It is hardly an eighth of a mile across," said Lynde. "You will find us waiting for you at the opposite end of the cut, unless you drive rapidly. It is more than a mile by the road."

"Do you wish to go, Ruth?"

Miss Denham hesitated an instant, and then answered by rising impulsively and giving her hand to Lynde. Evidently, her first intention had been to refuse. In a moment more she was standing beside him, and the carriage was lazily crawling up the hill with Mrs. Denham looking back through her glass at the cascade.

A dozen rude steps, partly artificial and partly formed by the strata of the limestone bank, led from the roadside up to the opening of the foot-way. For thirty or forty yards the fern-fringed path was too narrow to admit of two persons walking abreast. Miss Denham, with her skirts gathered in one hand, went first, picking her way over the small loose stones rendered slippery by the moss, and Lynde followed on in silence, hardly able to realize the success of the ruse which had come so near being a failure. His companion was equally preoccupied. Once she stopped for Lynde to detach her dress from a grasping twig, and once to pluck one of those pallid waxen flowers which sometimes dauntlessly find a footing even among the snowdrifts of the higher Alps. The air was full of the resinous breath of the pines, whose boughs, meeting and interlacing overhead, formed an arabesqued roof, through the openings of which the afternoon sunshine sifted, as if through stained glass. With the slender stems of the trees rising on each side in the semi-twilight, the grove was like the transept of a cathedral. It seemed a profanation to speak in such a place. Lynde could have wandered on forever in contented silence, with that tall, pliant figure in its severely cut drapery moving before him. As he watched the pure outline defining itself against the subdued light, he was reminded of a colored bas-relief he had seen on a certain Egyptian vase in the Museum at Naples. Presently the path widened, a brook babbled somewhere ahead among the rocks, and the grove abruptly ended. As Lynde stepped to Miss Denham's side he heaved a deep, involuntary sigh.

"What a sigh, Mr. Lynde!" she cried, swiftly turning upon him with a surprised smile. "It was scarcely complimentary."

"It was not exactly a compliment; it was an unpremeditated monody on the death of this day, which has flown too soon."

"You are very ready with your monody; it yet lacks three or four hours of sunset, when one might probably begin to lament. I am enjoying it all too much to have a regret."

"Do you know, I thought you were not enjoying it—the journey, I mean? You have not spoken a hundred words since we left Geneva."

"That was a proof of my perfect enjoyment, as you would know if you knew me better. Fine scenery always affects me like music, and, with Jessica, 'I am never merry when I hear sweet music.' Besides, Mr. Lynde, I was forming a plan."

"A plan?"

"A dark conspiracy"—

"Is the spirit of Lucretia Borgia present?"

—"in which you are to be chief conspirator, Mr. Lynde."

"Miss Denham, the person is dead, either by steel or poison; it is all one to me—I am equally familiar with both methods."

As the girl lifted up her eyes in a half-serious, half-amused way, and gave him a look in which gentleness and a certain shadow of hauteur were oddly blended, Lynde started in spite of himself. It was the very look of the poor little Queen of Sheba.

"With your bowl and dagger and monody," said Miss Denham, breaking into one of her rare laughs, "you are in full tragedy this afternoon. I am afraid my innocent plot will seem very tame to you in the face of such dreadful things."

"I promise beforehand to regard it as the one important matter in the world. What is it?"

"Nothing more than this: I want you to insist that aunt Gertrude and I ought to make the ascent of Montanvert and visit the Mer de Glace—before uncle Denham arrives."

"Why, would he object?"

"I do not think anything would induce him to trust either of us on one of those narrow mule-paths."

"But everybody goes up Montanvert as a matter of course. The bridle-way is perfectly safe."

"Uncle Denham once witnessed a painful accident on the Wetterhorn—indeed, he himself barely escaped death; and any suggestion of mountain climbing that cannot be done on wheels always meets a negative from him. I suspect my aunt will not strongly favor the proposal, but when I make it I shall depend on you to sustain me."

"I shall surely do so, Miss Denham. I have had this same excursion in my mind all along."

"I was wondering how I should get the chance to ask the favor of you, when that special Providence, which your friend Mr. Flemming pretends not to believe in, managed it for me."

"It wasn't I, then, but Providence, that invited you to walk?"

"It looks like it, Mr. Lynde."

"But at first you were disposed to reject the providential aid."

"I hesitated about leaving aunt Gertrude alone."

"If you had refused me, there would have been no end to my disappointment. This walk, though it is sixty or seventy miles too short, is the choicest thing in the whole journey."

"Come, Mr. Lynde, that is an improvement on your sigh."

"Does it occur to you that this is the first time we have chanced to be alone together, in all these weeks?"

"Yes," said Miss Ruth simply, "it is the first time."

"I am a great admirer of Mrs. Denham"—

"I do not see how you can help being; she is charming, and she likes you."

"But sometimes I have wished that—that Mr. Denham was here."

"Why?" asked Miss Ruth, regarding him full in the face.

"Because then, may be, she would have been less devoted to you."

Miss Denham did not reply for a moment.

"My aunt is very fond of me," she said gravely. "She never likes to have me absent an hour from her side."

"I can understand that," said Lynde, with an innocent air.

The girl glanced at him quickly, and went on: "She adopted me when I was only three years old; we have never been separated since. She lived in Paris all the time I was at school there, though she did not like Paris as a residence. She would make any sacrifice for me that a mother would make for a daughter. She has been mother and sister to me. I cannot overpay her devotion by any unselfishness of mine."

As she spoke, Lynde caught a hateful glimpse of the road through the stubby pine-trees beyond. It appeared to him only two minutes ago that he was assisting Miss Denham to mount the stone steps at the other extremity of the foot-path; and now he was to lose her again. She was with him alone for perhaps the last time.

"Miss Ruth!" said Lynde, with sudden earnestness in his voice. He had never before addressed her as Miss Ruth. She raised her eyes furtively to his face. "Miss Ruth"—

"Oh, there's the carriage, Mr. Lynde!" exclaimed Miss Denham, releasing the arm she had accepted a few paces back, and hurrying down the path, which here narrowed again as at the entrance to the grove. "And there is aunt Gertrude," she added, half turning to Lynde, with a rich bloom on her cheeks, "looking as distressed as if we had slipped over some precipice. But we have not, have we, Mr. Lynde?"

"No, we haven't slipped over any precipices," answered Lynde, with a curt laugh. "I wish we had," he muttered to himself. "She has dragged me through that grove and over those stones, and, without preventing me, has not permitted me to breathe the least word of love to her. I don't know how she did it. That girl's the most consummate coquette I ever saw. I am a child in her hands. I believe I'm beginning to be afraid of her."

Miss Ruth was already in the carriage, pinning the Alpine flower to the corsage of her aunt's dress, when Lynde reached the steps. Mrs. Denham's features expressed no very deep anxiety that he could discover. That was clearly a fiction of Miss Ruth's. Lynde resumed his place on the front seat, and the horses started forward. He was amused and vexed at the inconsequence of his interview with Miss Denham, and did not know whether to be wholly vexed or wholly amused. He had, at least, broken the ice, and it would be easier for him to speak when another opportunity offered. She had understood, and had not repulsed him; she had merely evaded him. Perhaps he had been guilty of a mismove in attempting to take her at a disadvantage. He was too discreet to dream of proposing any more walks. A short cut was plainly not the most direct way to reach Miss Denham.

She was in livelier spirits now than she had been in at any time during the day. "The exercise has done you good, Ruth," remarked Mrs. Denham; "I am sorry I did not accept Mr. Lynde's invitation myself." Mr. Lynde was also politely sorry, and Miss Ruth contributed her regrets with an emphasis that struck Lynde as malicious and overdone.

Shortly before arriving at St. Martin, Miss Ruth broached her Montanvert project, which, as she had prophesied, was coldly received by the aunt. Lynde hastened to assure Mrs. Denham that the ascent was neither dangerous nor difficult. Even guides were not necessary, though it was convenient to have them to lead the animals. On the way up there were excellent views of the Flegere and the Brevent. There was a capital inn at the summit, where they could lunch, and from the cliff behind the inn one could look directly down on the Mer de Glace. Then Lynde fell back upon his Murray and Baedeker. It was here that Professor Tyndall spent many weeks, at different times, investigating the theory of glacier motion; and the Englishman's hut, which Goethe mentions in his visit to the scene in 1779, was still standing. Miss Ruth begged with both eyes; the aunt wavered, and finally yielded. As a continuance of fine weather could not be depended on, it was agreed that they should undertake the ascent the following morning immediately after daybreak. Then the conversation drooped.

The magnificent scenery through which their route now wound began to absorb them. Here they crossed a bridge, spanning a purple chasm whose snake-like thread of water could be heard hissing among the sharp flints a hundred feet below; now they rattled through the street of a sleepy village that seemed to have no reason for being except its picturesqueness; now they were creeping up a tortuous steep gloomed by menacing crags; and now their way lingered for miles along a precipice, over the edge of which they could see the spear-like tips of the tall pines reaching up from the valley.

At the bridge between St. Martin and Sallanches the dazzling silver peaks of Mont Blanc, rising above the green pasturage of the Forclaz, abruptly revealed themselves to the travellers, who fancied for the moment that they were close upon the mountain. It was twelve miles away in a bee-line. From this point one never loses sight of those vast cones and tapering aiguilles. A bloom as delicate as that of the ungathered peach was gradually settling on all the fairy heights.

As the travellers drew nearer to the termination of their journey, they were less and less inclined to converse. At every turn of the sinuous road fresh splendors broke upon them. By slow degrees the glaciers became visible: first those of Gria and Taconay; then the Glacier des Boissons, thrusting a crook of steel-blue ice far into the valley; and then—faintly discernible in the distance, and seemingly a hand's breadth of snow framed by the sombre gorge—the Glacier des Bois, a frozen estuary of the Mer de Glace.

The twilight was now falling. For the last hour or more the three inmates of the carriage had scarcely spoken. They had unresistingly given themselves over to the glamour of the time and place. Along the ravines and in the lower gorges and chasms the gray dusk was gathering; high overhead the domes and pinnacles were each instant taking deeper tinges of rose and violet. It seemed as if a word loudly or carelessly uttered would break the spell of the alpgluhen. It was all like a dream, and it was in his quality of spectral figure in a dream that the driver suddenly turned on the box, and, pointing over his shoulder with the handle of his whip said—

"Chamouni!"

IX

MONTANVERT

The mist was still lingering in the valleys, though the remote peaks had been kindled more than an hour by the touch of sunrise. As Lynde paced up and down the trottoir in front of the Couronne hotel, he drew out his watch from time to time and glanced expectantly towards the hotel entrance. In the middle of the street stood a couple of guides, idly holding the bridles of three mules, two of which were furnished with side-saddles. It was nearly half an hour past the appointment, and the Denhams, who had retired at eight o'clock the night before in order to be fresh for an early start up the mountain, had made no sign. Lynde himself had set the lark an example that morning by breakfasting by candle-light. Here were thirty minutes lost. He quickened his pace up and down in front of the hotel, as if his own rapidity of movement would possibly exert some occult influence in hastening the loiterers; but another quarter of an hour dragged on without bringing them.

Lynde was impatiently consulting his watch for the twentieth time when Miss Denham's troubled face showed itself in the doorway.

"Isn't it too bad, Mr. Lynde? Aunt Gertrude can't go!"

"Can't go!" faltered Lynde.

"She has a headache from yesterday's ride. She got up, and dressed, but was obliged to lie down again."

"Then that's the end of it, I suppose," said Lynde despondently. He beckoned to one of the guides.

"I don't know," said Miss Denham, standing in an attitude of irresolution on the upper step, with her curved eyebrows drawn together like a couple of blackbirds touching bills. "I don't know what to do...she insists on our going. I shall never forgive myself for letting her see that I was disappointed. She added my concern for her illness to my regret about the excursion, and thought me more disappointed than I really was. Then she declared she would go in spite of her headache... unless I went."

The gloom which had overspread Lynde's countenance vanished.

"It is not one of her severest turns," continued Miss Ruth, ceasing to be a statue on a pedestal and slowly descending the hotel steps with her waterproof trailing from her left arm, "and she is quite capable of executing her threat. What shall we do, Mr. Lynde?"

"I think we had better try the mountain—for her sake," answered Lynde. "We need not attempt the Mer de Glace, you know; that can be left for another day. The ascent takes only two hours, the descent half an hour less; we can easily be back in time for lunch."

"Then let us do that."

Lynde selected the more amiable-looking of the two mules with side-saddles, dismissed one of the guides after a brief consultation, and helped Miss Denham to mount. In attending to these preliminaries Lynde had sufficient mastery over himself not to make any indecorous betrayal of his intense satisfaction at the turn affairs had taken. Fortune had given her into his hands for five hours! She should listen this time to what he had to say, though the mountain should fall.

At a signal from Lynde the remaining guide led the way at a brisk pace through the bustling town. In front of the various hotels were noisy groups of tourists about to set forth on pilgrimages, some bound for the neighboring glaciers and cascades, and others preparing for more distant and more hardy enterprises. It was a perfect Babel of voices—French, Scotch, German, Italian, and English; with notes of every sort of patois—above which the strident bass of the mules soared triumphantly at intervals. There are not many busier spots than Chamouni at early morning in the height of the season.

Our friends soon left the tumult and confusion behind them, and were skirting the pleasant meadows outside of the town. Passing by the way of the English church, they crossed to the opposite bank of the Arve, and in a few minutes gained the hamlet lying at the foot of Montanvert. Then the guide took the bridle of Miss Ruth's mule and the ascent began. The road stretches up the mountain in a succession of zigzags with sharp turns. Here and there the path is quarried out of the begrudging solid rock; in places the terrace is several yards wide and well wooded, but for the most part it is a barren shelf with a shaggy wall rising abruptly on one hand and a steep slope descending on the other. Higher up, these slopes become quite respectable precipices. A dozen turns, which were accomplished in unbroken silence, brought the party to an altitude of several hundred feet above the level.

"I—I don't know that I wholly like it," said Miss Ruth, holding on to the pommel of her saddle and looking down into the valley, checkered with fields and criss-crossed with shining rivulets. "Why do the mules persist in walking on the very edge?"

"That is a trick they get from carrying panniers. You are supposed to be a pannier, and the careful animal doesn't want to brush you off against the rocks. See this creature of mine; he has that hind hoof slipping over the precipice all the while. But he'll not slip; he's as sure-footed as a chamois, and has no more taste for tumbling off the cliff than you have. These mules are wonderfully intelligent. Observe how cautiously they will put foot on a loose stone, feeling all around it."

"I wish they were intelligent enough to be led in the middle of the path," said Miss Ruth, "but I suppose the guide knows."

"You may trust to him; he is a person of varied accomplishments, the chief of which is he doesn't understand a word of English. So you can scold, or say anything you like, without the least reserve. I picked him out for that," added Lynde, with a bland smile. "His comrade was a linguist."

"If I have anything disagreeable to say," replied Miss Ruth, with another bland smile, "I shall say it in French."

The guide, who spoke four languages, including English, never changed a muscle. Lynde, just before starting, had closely examined the two guides on their lingual acquirements—and retained the wrong man.

"I trust you will have no occasion, Miss Denham, to be anything but amiable, and that you will begin by granting me a favor. Will you?"

"Cela depend."

"There you go into French! I haven't offended you?"

"Oh, no. What is the favor?—in English."

"That you will let me call you Miss Ruth, instead of Miss Denham."

"I haven't the slightest objection, Mr. Lynde."

"And now I want you"—

"What, another favor?"

"Of course. Who ever heard of one favor?"

"To be sure! What is the second?"

"I want that you should be a little sorry when all this comes to an end."

"You mean when we leave Chamouni?"

"Yes."

"I shall be sorry then," said Miss Ruth frankly, "but I am not going to be sorry beforehand."

There was something very sweet to Lynde in her candor, but there was also something that restrained him for the moment from being as explicit as he had intended. He rode on awhile without speaking, watching the girl as the mule now and then turned the sharp angle of the path and began a new ascent. This movement always brought her face to face with him a moment— she on the grade above, and he below. Miss Ruth had grown accustomed to the novel situation, and no longer held on by the pommel of the saddle. She sat with her hands folded in her lap, pliantly lending herself to the awkward motion of the animal. Over her usual travelling-habit she had thrown the long waterproof which reached to her feet. As she sat there in a half-listless attitude, she was the very picture of the Queen of Sheba seated upon Deacon Twombly's mare. Lynde could not help seeing it; but he was schooling himself by degrees to this fortuitous resemblance. It was painful, but it was inevitable, and he would get used to it in time. "Perhaps," he mused, "if I had never had that adventure with the poor insane girl, I might not have looked twice at Miss Denham when we met—and loved her. It was the poor little queen who shaped my destiny, and I oughtn't to be ungrateful." He determined to tell the story to Miss Ruth some time when a fitting occasion offered.

It was only when the likeness flashed upon Lynde suddenly, as it had done in the grove the previous day, that it now had the power to startle him. At the present moment it did not even seriously annoy him. In an idle, pensive way he noted the coincidence of the man leading the mule. The man was Morton and the mule was Mary! Lynde smiled to himself at the reflection that Mary would probably not accept the analogy with very good grace if she knew about it. This carried him to Rivermouth; then he thought of Cinderella's slipper, packed away in the old hair-trunk in the closet, and how perfectly the slipper would fit one of those feet which a floating fold of the waterproof that instant revealed to him—and he was in Switzerland again.

"Miss Ruth," he said, looking up quickly and urging his mule as closely behind hers as was practicable, "what are your plans to be when your uncle comes?"

"When my uncle comes we shall have no plans—aunt Gertrude and I. Uncle Denham always plans for everybody."

"I don't imagine he will plan for me," said Lynde gloomily. "I wish he would, for I shall not know what to do with myself."

"I thought you were going to St. Petersburg."

"I have given that up."

"It's to be Northern Germany, then?"

"No, I have dropped that idea, too. Will Mr. Denham remain here any time?"

"Probably not long."

"What is to become of me after you are gone!" exclaimed Lynde. "When I think of Mr. Denham sweeping down on Chamouni to carry you off, I am tempted to drive this mule straight over the brink of one of these precipices!"

The girl leaned forward, looking at the rocky wall of the Flegere through an opening in the pines, and made no reply.

"Miss Ruth," said Lynde, "I must speak!"

"Do not speak," she said, turning upon him with a half-imperious, half-appealing gesture, "I forbid you;" and then, more gently, "We have four or five days, perhaps a week, to be together; we are true, frank friends. Let us be just that to the end."

"Those are mercifully cruel words," returned the young man, with a dull pain at his heart. "It is a sweet way of saying a bitter thing."

"It is a way of saying that your friendship is very dear to me, Mr. Lynde," she replied, sitting erect in the saddle, with the brightness and the blackness deepening in her eyes. "I wonder if I can make you understand how I prize it. My life has not been quite like that of other girls, partly because I have lived much abroad, and partly because I have been very delicate ever since my childhood; I had a serious lung trouble then, which has never left me. You would not think it, to look at me. Perhaps it is the anxiety I have given aunt Gertrude which has made her so tenacious of my affection that I have scarcely been permitted to form even those intimacies which girls form among themselves. I have never known any one—any gentleman—as intimately as I have known you. She has let me have you for my friend."

"But Miss Ruth"—

"Mr. Lynde," she said, interrupting him, "it was solely to your friendship that my aunt confided me to-day. I should be deceiving her if I allowed you to speak as—as you were speaking."

Lynde saw his mistake. He should have addressed himself in the first instance to the aunt. He had been lacking in proper regard for the convenances, forgetting that Ruth's education had been different from that of American girls. At home, if you love a girl you tell her so; over here, you go and tell her grandmother. Lynde dropped his head and remained silent, resolving to secure an interview with Mrs. Denham that night if possible. After a moment or two he raised his face. "Miss Ruth," said he, "if I had to choose, I would rather be your friend than any other woman's lover."

"That is settled, then," she returned, with heightened color. "We will not refer to this again;" and she brushed away a butterfly that was fluttering about her conceitedly in its new golden corselet.

Meanwhile the guide marched on stolidly with Ruth's reins thrown loosely over the crook of his elbow. In his summer courses up and down the mountain, the man, with his four languages, had probably assisted dumbly at much fugitive love-making and many a conjugal passage-at-arms. He took slight note of the conversation between the two young folks; he was clearly more interested in a strip of black cloud that had come within the half hour and hung itself over the Aiguille du Dru.

The foot-path and the bridle-road from Chamouni unite at the Caillet, a spring of fresh water halfway up the mountain. There the riders dismounted and rested five or six minutes at a rude hut perched like a brown bird under the cliff.

"I've the fancy to go on foot the rest of the distance," Lynde remarked, as he assisted Ruth into the saddle again.

"Then I'll let you lead the mule, if you will," said Ruth. "I'm not the least afraid."

"That is an excellent idea! Why did you not think of it sooner? I shall expect a buonamano, like a real guide, you know."

"I will give it you in advance," she said gayly, reaching forward and pretending to hold a coin between her thumb and finger.

Lynde caught her hand and retained it an instant, but did not dare to press it. He was in mortal fear of a thing which he could have crushed like a flower in his palm.

The young man drew the reins over his arm and moved forward, glancing behind him at intervals to assure himself that his charge was all right. As they approached the summit of the mountain the path took abrupter turns, and was crossed in numberless places by the channels of winter avalanches, which had mown down great pines as if they had been blades of grass. Here and there a dry water-course stretched like a wrinkle along the scarred face of the hill.

"Look at that, Miss Ruth!" cried Lynde, checking the mule and pointing to a slope far below them.

Nature, who loves to do a gentle thing even in her most savage moods, had taken one of those empty water-courses and filled it from end to end with forget-me-nots. As the wind ruffled the millions of petals, this bed of flowers, only a few inches wide but nearly a quarter of a mile in length, looked like a flashing stream of heavenly blue water rushing down the mountain side.

By and by the faint kling-kling of a cowbell sounding far up the height told the travellers that they were nearing the plateau. Occasionally they descried a herdsman's chalet, pitched at an angle against the wind on the edge of an arete, or clinging like a wasp's-nest to some jutting cornice of rock. After making four or five short turns, the party passed through a clump of scraggy, wind-swept pines, and suddenly found themselves at the top of Montanvert.

A few paces brought them to the Pavilion, a small inn kept by the guide Couttet. Here the mules were turned over to the hostler, and Miss Ruth and Lynde took a quarter of an hour's rest, examining the collection of crystals and moss-agates and horn-carvings which M. Couttet has for show in the apartment that serves him as salon, cafe, and museum. Then the two set out for the rocks overlooking the glacier.

The cliff rises precipitously two hundred and fifty feet above the frozen sea, whose windings can be followed, for a distance of five miles, to the walls of the Grandes and Petites Jorasses. Surveyed from this height, the Mer de Glace presents the appearance of an immense ploughed field covered by a fall of snow that has become dingy. The peculiar corrugation of the surface is scarcely discernible, and one sees nothing of the wonderful crevasses, those narrow and often fathomless partings of the ice, to look into which is like looking into a split sapphire. The first view from the cliff is disappointing, but presently the marvel of it all assails and possesses one.

"I should like to go down on the ice," said Ruth, after regarding the scene for several minutes in silence.

"We must defer that to another day," said Lynde. "The descent of the moraine from this point is very arduous, and is seldom attempted by ladies. Besides, if we do anything we ought to cross the glacier and go home by the way of the Mauvais Pas. We will do that yet. Let us sit upon this boulder and talk."

"What shall we talk about? I don't feel like talking."

"I'll talk to you. I don't know of what... I will tell you a story."

"A story, Mr. Lynde? I like stories as if I were only six years old. But I don't like those stories which begin with 'Once there was a little girl,' who always turns out to be the little girl that is listening."

"Mine is not of that kind," replied Lynde, with a smile, steadying Miss Ruth by the hand as she seated herself on the boulder; "and yet it touches on you indirectly. It all happened long ago."

"It concerns me, and happened long ago? I am interested already. Begin!"

"It was in the summer of 1872. I was a clerk in a bank then, at Rivermouth, and the directors had given me a vacation. I hired a crazy old horse and started on a journey through New Hampshire. I didn't have any destination; I merely purposed to ride on and on until I got tired, and then ride home again. The weather was beautiful, and for the first three or four days I never enjoyed myself better in my life. The flowers were growing, the birds were singing—the robins in the sunshine and the whippoorwills at dusk—and the hours were not long enough for me. At night I slept in a tumble-down barn, or anywhere, like a born tramp. I had a mountain brook for a wash-basin and the west wind for a towel. Sometimes I invited myself to a meal at a farm-house when there wasn't a tavern handy; and when there wasn't any farm-house, and I was very hungry, I lay down under a tree and read in a book of poems."

"Oh, that was just delightful!" said Ruth, knitting the fingers of both hands over one knee and listening to him with a child-like abandon which Lynde found bewitching.

"On the fourth day—there are some persons crossing on the ice," said Lynde, interrupting himself.

"Never mind the persons on the ice!"

"On the fourth day I came to a wild locality among the Ragged Mountains, where there was not a human being nor a house to be seen. I had got up before breakfast was ready that morning, and I was quite anxious to see the smoke curling up from some kitchen chimney. Here, as I mounted a hill-side, the saddle-girth broke, and I jumped off to fix it. Somehow, I don't know precisely how, the horse gave a plunge, jerked the reins out of my hands, and started on a dead run for Rivermouth."

"That wasn't very pleasant," suggested Ruth.

"Not a bit. I couldn't catch the animal, and I had the sense not to try. I climbed to the brow of the hill and was not sorry to see a snug village lying in the valley."

"What village was that?"

"I don't know to this day—with any certainty. I didn't find out then, and afterwards I didn't care to learn. Well, I shouldered my traps and started for the place to procure another horse, not being used to going under the saddle myself. I had a hard time before I got through; but that I shall not tell you about. On my way to the village I met a young girl. This young girl is the interesting part of the business."

"She always is, you know."

"She was the most beautiful creature I had ever seen—up to that time. She was dressed all in white, and looked like an angel. I expected she would spread wing and vanish before I could admire her half enough; but she did not. The moment she saw me she walked straight to the spot where I stood, and looked me squarely in the face."

"Wasn't that rather rude—for an angel?"

"You wouldn't have thought so. She did it like a young goddess with the supreme prerogative to flash herself that way on mortals by the roadside."

"Oh, she was a young goddess as well as an angel."

"After she had looked me in the eye a second," continued Lynde, not heeding the criticism, "she said—what do you suppose she said?"

"How can I imagine?"

"You could not, in a thousand years. Instead of saying, 'Good-morning, sir,' and dropping me a courtesy, she made herself very tall and said, with quite a grand air, 'I am the Queen of Sheba!' Just fancy it. Then she turned on her heel and ran up the road."

"Oh, that was very rude. Is this a true story, Mr. Lynde?"

"That is the sad part of it, Miss Ruth. This poor child had lost her reason, as I learned subsequently. She had wandered out of an asylum in the neighborhood. After a while some men came and took her back again—on my horse, which they had captured in the road."

"The poor, poor girl! I am sorry for her to the heart. Your story began like a real romance; is that all of it! It is sad enough."

"That is all. Of course I never saw her afterwards."

"But you remembered her, and pitied her?"

"For a long time, Miss Ruth."

"I like you for that. But what has this to do with me? You said"—

"The story touched on you indirectly?"

"Yes."

"Well, so it does; I will tell you how. This poor girl was beautiful enough in your own fashion to be your sister, and when I first saw you"—

"Monsieur," said the guide, respectfully lifting a forefinger to his hat as he approached, "I think it looks like rain."

The man had spoken in English. Ruth went crimson to the temples, and Lynde's face assumed a comical expression of dismay.

"Looks like rain," he repeated mechanically. "I thought you told me you did not understand English."

"Monsieur is mistaken. It is Jean Macquart that does not spik English."

"Very well," said Lynde; "if it is going to rain we had better be moving. It would not be pleasant to get blockaded up here by a storm—or rather it would! Are the animals ready?"

"They are waiting at the foot of the path, monsieur."

Lynde lost no time getting Ruth into the saddle, and the party began their descent, the guide again in charge of the girl's mule. On the downward journey they unavoidably faced the precipices, and the road appeared to them much steeper than when they ascended.

"Is it wind or rain, do you think?" asked Lynde, looking at a wicked black cloud that with angrily curled white edges was lowering itself over the valley.

"I think it is both, monsieur."

"How soon?"

"I cannot know. Within an hour, surely."

"Perhaps we were wrong to attempt going down," said Lynde.

"Monsieur might be kept at Couttet's one, two—three days. But, if monsieur wishes, I will go on and tell the friends of mademoiselle that you are detained."

"Oh, no!" cried Ruth, filled with horror at the suggestion. "We MUST return. I shall not mind the rain, if it comes."

As she spoke, a loose handful of large drops rustled through the pine-boughs overhead, and softly dashed themselves against the rocks.

"It has come," said Lynde.

"I have my waterproof," returned the girl. "I shall do very well. But you"—

The sentence was cut short by a flash of lightning, followed by a heavy peal of thunder that rolled through the valley and reverberated for one or two minutes among the hills. The guide grasped the reins close up to the bits, and urged the mule forward at a brisk trot. The sky cleared, and for a moment it looked as if the storm had drifted elsewhere; but the party had not advanced twenty paces before there was a strange rustling sound in the air, and the rain came down. The guide whipped off a coarse woollen coat he wore, and threw it over the girl's shoulders, tying it by the sleeves under her chin.

"Oh, you must not do that!" she cried, "you will catch your death!"

"Mademoiselle," he replied, laughing, as he gave another knot to the sleeves, "for thirty-eight years, man and boy, I have been rained upon and snowed upon—and voila!"

"You're a fine fellow, my friend, if you do speak English," cried Lynde, "and I hope some honest girl has found it out before now."

"Monsieur," returned the man, signing himself with the cross, "she and the little one are in heaven."

The rain came down in torrents; it pattered like shot against the rocks; it beat the air of the valley into mist. Except the path immediately before them, and the rocky perpendicular wall now on their right and now on their left, the travellers could distinguish nothing through the blinding rain. Shortly the wind began to blow, whistling in the stiff pines as it whistles among the taut cordage of a ship in a gale. At intervals it tore along the salient zigzags and threatened to sweep the mules off their legs. The flashes of lightning now followed one another in rapid succession, and the thunder crashed incessantly through the gorges. It appeared as if the great cones and cromlechs were tumbling pell-mell from every direction into the valley.

Though the situation of the three persons on the mountain side was disagreeable to the last extent, they were exposed to only one especial danger—that from a land-slide or a detached boulder. At every ten steps the guide glanced up the dripping steep, and listened. Even the mules were not without a prescience of this peril. The sharpest lightning did not make them wince, but at the faintest sound of a splinter of rock or a pebble rustling down the slope, their ears instantly went forward at an acute angle. The footing soon became difficult on account of the gullies formed by the rain. In spite of his anxiety concerning Ruth, Lynde could not help admiring the skill with which the sagacious animals felt their way. Each fore hoof as it touched the earth seemed endowed with the sense of fingers.

Lynde had dismounted after the rain set in and was walking beside the girl's mule. Once, as an unusually heavy clap of thunder burst over their heads, she had impulsively stretched out her hand to him; he had taken it, and still held it, covered by a fold of the waterproof, steadying her so. He was wet to the skin, but Ruth's double wraps had preserved her thus far from anything beyond the dampness.

"Are you cold?" he asked. Her hand was like ice.

"Not very," she replied in a voice rendered nearly inaudible by a peal of thunder that shook the mountain. A ball of crimson fire hung for a second in the murky sky and then shot into the valley. The guide glanced at Lynde, as much as to say, "That struck."

They were rapidly leaving the wind above them; its decrease was noticeable as they neared the Caillet. The rain also had lost its first fury, and was falling steadily. Here and there bright green patches of the level plain showed themselves through the broken vapors. Ruth declined to halt at the Caillet; her aunt would be distracted about her, and it was better to take advantage of the slight lull in the storm, and push on. So they stopped at the hut only long enough for Lynde to procure a glass of cognac, a part of which he induced the girl to drink. Then they resumed their uncomfortable march.

When Lynde again looked at his companion he saw that her lips were purple, and her teeth set. She confessed this time to being very cold. The rain had at length penetrated the thick wrappings and thoroughly chilled her. Lynde was in despair, and began bitterly to reproach himself for having undertaken the excursion without Mrs. Denham. Her presence could not have warded off the storm, but it would have rendered it possible for the party to postpone their descent until pleasant weather. Undoubtedly it had been his duty to leave Miss Ruth at the inn and return alone to Chamouni. He had not thought of that when the guide made his suggestion. There was now nothing to do but to hurry.

The last part of the descent was accomplished at a gait which offered the cautious mules no chance to pick their steps. Lynde's animal, left to its own devices, was following on behind, nibbling the freshened grass. But the road was not so rough, and the stretches protected by the trees were in good condition. In less than three quarters of an hour from the half-way hut, the party were at the foot of the mountain, where they found a close carriage which Mrs. Denham had thoughtfully sent to meet them. Benumbed with the cold and cramped by riding so long in one position, the girl was unable to stand when she was lifted from the saddle. Lynde carried her to the carriage and wrapped her in a heavy afghan that lay on the seat. They rode to the hotel without exchanging a word. Lynde was in too great trouble, and Ruth was too exhausted to speak. She leaned back with her eyes partially closed, and did not open them until the carriage stopped. Mrs. Denham stood at the hall door.

"Mr. Lynde! Mr. Lynde!" she said, taking the girl in her arms.

The tone of reproach in her voice cut him to the quick.

"He was in no way to blame, aunt," said Ruth, trying to bring a smile to her blanched face; "it was I who WOULD go." She reached back her hand unperceived by Mrs. Denham and gave it to Lynde. He raised it gratefully to his lips, but as he relinquished it and turned away he experienced a sudden, inexplicable pang—as if he had said farewell to her.

X

IN THE SHADOW OF MONT BLANC

By the time Lynde had changed his wet clothing, the rain had turned into a dull drizzle, which folded itself like a curtain about the valley. Mont Blanc, with its piled-up acres of desolation, loomed through the mist, a shapeless, immeasurable cloud, within whose shadow the little town was to live darkly, half blotted out, for the next four days.

Lynde spent the afternoon between his own chamber and the reading-room of the hotel, wandering restlessly from one to the other, and not venturing to halt at Mrs. Denham's door to inquire after Ruth. Though he held himself nearly guiltless in what had occurred, Mrs. Denham's rebuking tone and gesture had been none the less intolerable. He was impatient to learn Ruth's condition, and was growing every moment more anxious as he reflected on her extreme delicacy and the severe exposure she had undergone; but he could not bring himself just then to go to Mrs. Denham for information. He concluded to wait until he met her at dinner; but Mrs. Denham did not come down to the table d'hote.

The twilight fell earlier than usual, and the long evening set in. Lynde smoked his cigar gloomily at an open window looking upon the street. It was deserted and dismal. Even the shop across the way, where they sold alpenstocks and wood-carvings and knick-knacks in polished lapis, was empty; in pleasant weather the shop was always crowded with curiosity-mongers. The raw wind spitefully blew the rain into Lynde's face as he looked out. "Quel temps de loup!" sighed a polite little French gentleman, making his unlighted cigarette an excuse for addressing Lynde. The wretched little French gentleman was perishing with a desire to say a thousand graceful things to somebody, but Lynde was in no mood for epigrams. He gave his interlocutor a light, and sheered off. In a corner of the reading-room was a tattered collection of Tauchnitz novels; Lynde picked up one and tried to read, but the slim types ran together and conveyed no meaning to him. It was becoming plain that he was to have no communication with the Denhams that night unless he assumed the initiative. He pencilled a line on the reverse of a visiting card and sent it up to Mrs. Denham's parlor. The servant returned with the card on his waiter. The ladies had retired. Then Lynde took himself off to bed disconsolately.

It was nearly nine o'clock when he awoke the following morning. The storm had not lifted; the colorless clouds were still letting down a fine, vapory rain that blurred everything. As soon as he had breakfasted, Lynde went to Mrs. Denham's rooms. She answered his knock in person and invited him by a silent gesture to enter the parlor. He saw by the drawn expression of her countenance that she had not slept.

"Ruth is ill," she said in a low voice, replying to Lynde's inquiry.

"You do not mean very ill?"

"I fear so. She has passed a dreadful night. I have had a doctor."

"Is it as serious as that? What does he say?"

"He says it is a severe cold, with symptoms of pneumonia; but I do not think he knows," returned Mrs. Denham despairingly. "I must despatch a courier to my husband; our old family physician is now with him at Paris. I have just received a letter, and they are not coming this week! They must come at once. I do not know how to telegraph them, as they are about to change their hotel. Besides, I believe a telegram cannot be sent from here; the nearest office is at Geneva. I must send some messenger who will have intelligence enough to find Mr. Denham wherever he is."

"I will go."

"You?"

"Why not? I shall waste less time than another. There should be no mistake in the delivery of this message. A courier might get drunk, or be stupid. I can do nothing here. If it had not been for me, possibly this unfortunate thing would not have happened. I am determined to go, whether you consent or not."

"I shall be grateful to you all my life, Mr. Lynde. I should not have thought of asking such a favor. Ruth says I was rude to you yesterday. I did not mean to be. I was distracted with anxiety at having her out in such a storm. If there is any blame in the matter it is entirely mine. You forgive me?"

"There is nothing to forgive, Mrs. Denham; blame rests on no one; neither you nor I could foresee the rain. Write a line to Mr. Denham while I pack my valise; I shall be ready in ten minutes. Who is his banker at Paris?"

"I think he has none."

"How do you address your letters?"

"I have written but once since Mr. Denham's arrival, and then I directed the letter to the Hotel Walther."

"He has probably left his new address there. However, I shall have no difficulty in finding him. Mrs. Denham"—Lynde hesitated.

"Mr. Lynde?"

"Can I not see her a moment?"

"See Ruth?"

"My request appears strange to you, does it not? It would not appear strange if you knew all."

"All? I don't understand you," replied Mrs. Denham, resting her hand on the back of a chair and regarding him with slowly dilating pupils.

"If you knew how troubled I am—and how deeply I love her."

"You love Ruth!"

"More than I can tell you."

"Have you told HER?" Mrs. Denham demanded.

"Not in so many words."

Mrs. Denham slowly sank into the chair and for several seconds appeared completely oblivious of the young man's presence; then, turning sharply on Lynde, and half rising, she asked with a kind of fierceness, "Does Ruth know it?"

"A woman always knows when she is loved, I fancy. Miss Denham probably knew it before I did."

Mrs. Denham made an impatient gesture and subsided into the chair again. She remained silent a while, staring at the pattern of the carpet at her feet.

"Mr. Lynde," she said at length, "I was not prepared for this. The possibility that you might grow interested in my niece naturally occurred to me at first. I was pleased when I became convinced that the acquaintance between you had resolved itself into merely a friendly liking. I was thrown off my guard by your seemingly frank manner. I trusted you. You have been alone with my niece but twice—once for only ten minutes. I will do you the justice to say that you have made the most of those two occasions."

"I made very little of those two occasions," said Lynde reflectively.

"I think you have been—treacherous!"

"I do not see what there can be of treachery in my admiring Miss Denham," he replied, with a flush. "I entered into no compact not to admire her."

"Mr. Lynde, Mr. Denham will not approve of this."

"Not at first, perhaps...but afterwards?"

"Neither now nor afterwards, Mr. Lynde."

"Why not?"

"He has other views for Ruth," said Mrs. Denham coldly.

"Other views!" repeated Lynde, paling. "I thought her free."

"She is not free in that sense."

The assertion Ruth had made to him the previous day on the mountain side, to the effect that she had never known any gentleman as intimately as she had known him, flashed across Lynde's memory. If Mr. Denham had views for her, certainly Ruth was either ignorant of them or opposed to them.

"Is Miss Ruth aware of Mr. Denham's intentions regarding her?"

"I must decline to answer you, Mr. Lynde," said Mrs. Denham, rising with something like haughtiness in her manner.

"You are right. I was wrong to speak at present. I cannot conceive what impelled me; it was neither the time nor the place. I beg you to consider everything unsaid, if you can, and I especially beg you not to mention this conversation in your note to Mr. Denham. The one important thing now is to have proper medical attendance for your niece. The rest will take care of itself."

Lynde bowed somewhat formally and was turning away, when Mrs. Denham laid her fingers lightly on the sleeve of his coat. "I am sorry I have pained you," she said, as if with a touch of remorse.

"I confess I am pained," he replied, with the faintest smile, "but I am not discouraged, Mrs. Denham."

A quarter of an hour later Lynde was on the way to Geneva. Life and the world had somehow darkened for him within the hour. It seemed to him incredible that that was the same road over which he had passed so joyously two days before. The swollen torrents now rushed vengefully through the arches of the stone bridges; the low-hanging opaque clouds pressed the vitality out of the atmosphere; in the melancholy gray light the rain-soaked mountains wore a human aspect of dolor. He was not sorry when the mist gathered like frost on the carriage windows and shut the landscape from his sight.

The storm had been terrible in Geneva and in the neighborhood. It was a scene of devastation all along the road approaching the town. Most of the trees in the suburbs had been completely stripped of foliage by the hailstones; the leaves which still clung to the bent twigs were slit as if volleys of buckshot had been fired into them. But the saddest thing to see was field after field of rich grain mown within a few inches of the ground by those swift, keen sickles which no man's hand had held. In the section of the city through which Lynde passed to the railroad the streets were literally strewn with broken tiles and chimney-pots. In some places the brown and purple fragments lay ankle-deep, like leaves in autumn. Hundreds of houses had been unroofed and thousands of acres laid waste in a single night. It will take the poor of the canton fifty years to forget the summer storm of 1875.

By noon the next day Lynde was in Paris. As he stepped from the station and stood under the blue sky in the sparkling Parisian atmosphere, the gloom and desolation he had left behind at Geneva and Chamouni affected him like the remembrance of a nightmare. For a brief space he forgot his sorrowful errand; then it came back to him with its heaviness redoubled by the contrast. He threw his valise on the seat of a fiacre standing near the crossway, and drove to the office of Galignani in the Rue de Rivoli—the morgue in which the names of all foreign travellers are daily laid out for recognition. The third name Lynde fell upon was that of William Denham, Hotel Meurice. The young man motioned to the driver to follow him and halt at the hotel entrance, which was only a few steps further in the arcade facing the gardens of the Tuileries.

Mr. Denham was at breakfast in the small salon opening on the paved square formed by the four interior walls of the building; he had just seated himself at the table, which was laid for two persons, when the waiter brought him Mrs. Denham's note and Lynde's card. Mr. Denham glanced from one to the other, and then broke the seal of the envelope with a puzzled air which directly changed into a perturbed expression.

"Show the gentleman in here," he said, speaking over the top of the note-sheet to the servant, "and set another cover."

It was a strongly featured person of fifty or fifty-five, slightly bald, and closely shaven with the exception of a heavy iron-gray mustache, who rose from the chair and stepped forward to meet Lynde as he entered. Lynde's name was familiar to Mr. Denham, it having figured rather prominently in his wife's correspondence during the latter part of the sojourn at Geneva.

"You have placed us all under deep obligations to you, sir," said Mr. Denham, with a smile in which the severity of his features melted.

"The obligations are on my side, sir," replied Lynde. "I owe Mrs. Denham a great many kindnesses. I wish I could have found some happier way than the present to express my sense of them."

"I sincerely hope she was not justified in allowing you to take this long journey. I beg of you to tell me what has happened. Mrs. Denham has been anything but explicit."

She had merely announced Ruth's illness, leaving it to Lynde to inform Mr. Denham of the particulars. That gentleman wrinkled his brows involuntarily as he listened to Lynde's account of his mountain excursion alone with Ruth and the result. "I have not seen Miss Denham since," said Lynde, concluding his statement, in which he had tripped and stumbled woefully. "I trust that Mrs. Denham's anxiety has exaggerated her niece's condition."

"Ruth is far from strong," replied Mr. Denham, "and my wife is almost morbidly quick to take alarm about her. In fact, we both are. Do you know how the trains run to Geneva? Is there anything earlier than the evening express?"

Lynde did not know.

"We will ascertain after breakfast," continued Mr. Denham. "Of course you have not breakfasted yet. You ought to be in appetite by this time. I am unusually late myself, this morning, and my friend, the doctor, is still later.

We tired ourselves out yesterday in a jaunt to Fontainebleau. The doctor's an incorrigible sightseer. Ah, there he is! Mr. Lynde, my friend, Dr. Pendegrast."

Lynde did not start at hearing this unexpected name, though it pierced his ear like a sharp-pointed arrow. He was paralyzed for an instant; a blur came over his eyes, and he felt that his hands and feet were turning into ice However, he made an effort to rise and salute the elderly gentleman who stood at his side with a hand stretched out in the cordial American fashion.

Evidently Dr. Pendegrast did not recognize Lynde, in whose personal appearance three years had wrought many changes. The doctor himself had altered in no essential; he was at that period of man's life—between fifty and sixty—when ravaging time seems to give him a respite for a couple of lustrums. As soon as Lynde could regain his self-possession he examined Dr. Pendegrast with the forlorn hope that this was not HIS Dr. Pendegrast; but it was he, with those round eyes like small blue-faience saucers, and that slight, wiry figure. If any doubt had lingered in the young man's mind, it would have vanished as the doctor drew forth from his fob that same fat little gold watch, and turned it over on its back in the palm of his hand, just as he had done the day he invited Lynde to remain and dine with him at the asylum.

"Why, bless me, Denham!" he exclaimed, laying his ear to the crystal of the time-piece as if he were sounding a doubtful lung, "my watch has run down— a thing that hasn't happened these twenty years." As he stood with his head inclined on one side, the doctor's cheery eyes inadvertently rested upon Mr. Denham's face and detected its unwonted disturbance.

"Mr. Lynde has just come from Chamouni," said Mr. Denham, answering the doctor's mute interrogation. "It seems that Ruth is ill."

Dr. Pendegrast glanced at Lynde and turned to Mr. Denham again.

"I imagine it is only a cold," Mr. Denham continued. "She was caught in a rain-storm on the mountain and got very wet. Mrs. Denham is of course worried about her, and Mr. Lynde has been kind enough to come all the way to Paris for us."

"That WAS very kind in him."

Dr. Pendegrast drew a chair up to the table and began questioning Lynde. Beyond satisfying such of the doctor's inquiries as he could, Lynde did not speak during the meal. He managed to swallow a cup of black coffee, which revived him; but he was unable to eat a mouthful. The intelligence he had brought so occupied his companions that the young man's very noticeable agitation and constraint escaped them. In a few minutes Mr. Denham rose from his seat and begged the two gentlemen to finish their breakfast at leisure, while he went to consult the time-table at the bureau of the hotel.

"The doctor can give you a genuine Havana," he remarked to Lynde. "I will join you shortly in the smoking-room."

While Dr. Pendegrast silently drank his coffee, Lynde pieced his scattered thoughts together. What course should he pursue? Should he take the doctor into his confidence, or should he let himself drift? How could the doctor help him in the circumstances? Ruth had been insane. What could do away with that dreadful fact, the revelation of which now appalled him as if he had never suspected it. Ruth, Ruth—the very name was significant of calamity! Flemming's words rang in his ears: "You would not marry her!" He had not replied to Flemming that night when the case was merely supposititious. But now—it seemed to Lynde that he had never loved Ruth until this moment. The knowledge of her misfortune had added to his love that great pity of which he had spoken to his friend. But could he marry her? He did not dare put the question squarely, for he dared not confess to himself that he could not give her up. This, then, was the key to Mrs. Denham's cold rejection of his suit; it explained, also, Ruth's unwillingness to have him speak to her of his love. How poignant must have been her anguish that day on Montanvert if she cared for him! She loved him—how could he doubt it?—but she had accepted the hopelessness of the position. In his own mind he had accused her of coquetry in their walk at the cascade of Nant d'Arpenaz. He saw through it all now; the scales had fallen from his eyes. She was hiding her misery under a smooth face, as women will. A sudden reflection sent a chill over Lynde; what if she had recognized him that first day at dinner in Geneva and had been playing a part all the while! Then she was the most subtile actress that ever lived, and the leading lady of the Theatre Francais might indeed go and take lessons of her, as Flemming had said. The thought gave Lynde a shock. He would not like to have the woman he loved such an actress as that. Had Ruth revealed everything to the aunt, and was she too playing a part? In her several allusions to Dr. Pendegrast Mrs. Denham had called him "the doctor" simply, or "an old friend of our family," and never once pronounced his name. "Was that accidental or intentional?" Lynde wondered. "It was inevitable that he and I should meet sooner or later. Was she endeavoring to keep the knowledge of Dr. Pendegrast from me as long as possible? The exigency has unmasked her!"

"Now, Mr. Lynde, I am at your service."

Lynde gave a start, as if the doctor had suddenly dropped down at his side from out of the sky.

Dr. Pendegrast pushed back his chair and led the way across the quadrangle, in which a number of persons were taking coffee at small tables set here and there under oleander-trees in green-painted tubs. The smoking-room was unoccupied. Lynde stood a moment undetermined in the centre of the apartment, and then he laid his hand on the doctor's shoulder.

"You don't remember me?"

"Ah, then I HAVE seen you before!" exclaimed Dr. Pendegrast, transfixed in the act of drawing a cigar from his case. "Your name and your face puzzled me, but I could not place you, so I didn't mention it. You must pardon an old man's bad memory. I am confused. When and where have I had the pleasure of seeing you?"

"It was scarcely a pleasure," said Lynde, with bitterness.

"Indeed! I cannot imagine that; it is a pleasure now," returned the doctor courteously. "It was three years ago, at your asylum. As you will recollect, I was brought there by mistake the day the patients"—

"Bless me!" exclaimed the doctor, dropping the ignited match. "How could I forget you! I took such a great liking to you, too. I have thought of that awkward affair a thousand times. But, really, coming across you in this unexpected manner"—

"I suppose I have changed somewhat," Lynde broke in. "Dr. Pendegrast, I am in a very strange position here. It is imperative you should be perfectly frank with me. You will have to overlook my abruptness. Mr. Denham may return any instant, and what I have to say cannot be said in his presence. I know that Miss Denham has been under your charge as a patient. I want to know more than that bare circumstance."

The doctor recoiled a step. "Of course," he said, recovering himself, "you must have recognized her."

"I met your friends six or seven weeks ago at Geneva," continued Lynde. "I recognized Miss Denham at once; but later I came to doubt and finally to disbelieve that I had ever seen her elsewhere. I refused to accept the testimony of my eyes and ears because—because so much of my happiness depended on my rejecting it."

"Does Mrs. Denham know that you are in possession of the fact you mention? Denham of course doesn't."

"No; it is my meeting with you that he turned my discarded doubt into a certainty."

"Then, I beg of you," said Dr. Pendegrast throwing a glance across the quadrangle, "not to breathe a syllable of this; do not even think of it. It has been kept from every one—from even the most intimate friends of the family; Ruth herself is not aware of her temporary derangement."

"Miss Denham does not know it?"

"She has not the remotest suspicion of the misfortune which befell her three years ago."

"Miss Denham does not know it?" repeated Lynde in a dazed way. "That—that seems impossible! Pardon me. How did it happen, Dr. Pendegrast?"

"I assume that you are not asking me through idle curiosity," said the doctor, looking at him attentively.

"I have vital reasons for my question, Doctor."

"I do not see why I should not tell you, since you know so much. The family were in Florida that spring. Ruth had not been well for several months; they had gone South on her account. It was partly a pulmonary difficulty. On their return North, Ruth was prostrated by a typhoid fever. She recovered from that but with her mind strangely disordered. The mental malady increased with her convalescence. Denham and I were old friends; he had faith in my skill, and she was placed in my care. She was brought to the asylum because I could not attend to her anywhere else. I considered her case serious at first, even hopeless. The human body is still a mystery, after science has said its last word. The human mind is a deeper mystery. While I doubted of her recovery, she recovered. At the first intimation of returning health, she was taken home; when her wandering thought came back to her she was in her own room. She remembered that she had been very ill, a long time ill; she had a faint impression that I had attended her meanwhile; but she remembered nothing more. The knowledge of her affliction was kept a secret from her— unwisely, I think. They put it off and put it off, until it became very awkward to tell her."

Lynde started as he recalled his conversation with Miss Denham on the rocks overhanging the Mer de Glace. With unwitting cruelty he had told Ruth her own pathetic story, and she had unconsciously pitied herself! A lump came into his throat as he remembered it.

"That was a mistake," said Lynde, with an effort, "not to tell her."

"An absurd mistake. It has given my friends no end of trouble and embarrassment."

"How long was she afflicted this way?"

"Something less than two months."

"It was the result of the fever?"

"That chiefly."

"It was not—hereditary?" Lynde lingered on the word.

"No."

"Then it is not likely to occur again?"

"I cannot think of anything more unlikely," returned the doctor, "unless the same conditions conspire, which is scarcely supposable, as I could easily prove to you. You can understand, Mr. Lynde, that this has been a sore trial to Denham and his wife; they have had no children, and their hearts are bound up in Ruth. The dread of a recurrence of the trouble has haunted them night and day in spite of all the arguments I could advance to reassure them. They have got what our French friends call a fixed idea, which is generally an idea that requires a great deal of fixing. The girl ought to marry—every woman ought to marry, it is her one mission; but between their affections and their apprehensions, my friends have allowed Ruth no opportunity to form attachments."

"I'm glad of that," said Lynde quietly.

"Are you!" snapped the doctor. "I am not. I would like to see her married some day. Meanwhile I would like to see a dozen lovers about her. It is as natural for a young girl to coquet as it is for a canary to peck at its seed or trim its bill on a bit of fishbone. It is had for the girl and the canary when they are prevented."

"There is something human in this crisp old doctor," said Lynde to himself, and then aloud: "So Mr. Denham has no matrimonial plans for her?"

"None whatever. Since Ruth's recovery the family have been constantly on the wing, either at home or abroad. Most of Ruth's life has been passed over here. I trust to your discretion. You will perceive the necessity of keeping all this to yourself."

"I do, and I now see that your travelling with the Denhams is a circumstance in no way connected with the state of Miss Denham's health."

"Not in the most distant manner, Mr. Lynde. I am with them because they are my old friends. I was worn out with professional work, and I ran across the sea to recuperate. It is fortunate I did, since Ruth chances to need me."

Lynde pondered a moment, and then asked abruptly: "Does Mrs. Denham know of my former meeting with her niece?"

"I never breathed a word to Mrs. Denham on the subject of Ruth's escapade," replied the doctor. "It would have pained her without mending matters. Besides, I was not proud of that transaction."

Mrs. Denham's suppression of the doctor's name, then, in speaking of him to Lynde, had been purely accidental.

"Miss Ruth's strange hallucination, in her illness, as to personality, her fancy about the Queen of Sheba—what was that traceable to?" asked Lynde, after a pause.

"Heaven only knows. She was reading the Old Testament very much in those days. I have sometimes accepted that as an explanation. It often happens that a delusion takes its cue from something read, or thought, or experienced in a rational state. In the case of the man Blaisdell, for example—you remember him, with his marble ship? He was formerly an enterprising ship-builder; during the Southern war he filled a contract with government for a couple of ironclads, and made his fortune. The depression in shipping afterwards ruined him—and he fell to constructing marble vessels! He is dead, by the way. I wonder if his reason has been given back to him—in that other world."

Lynde did not speak immediately, and the doctor relighted his cigar, which had gone out.

"Dr. Pendegrast, you have lifted a crushing weight from me. I cannot explain it to you now and here; but you shall know some day."

Dr. Pendegrast smiled. "I didn't recollect you at first, Mr. Lynde; my memory for names and faces is shockingly derelict, but I have retained most of my other faculties in tolerably good order. I have been unreserved with you because I more than suspect"—

The doctor's sentence was cut short by Mr. Denham, who entered at the instant. He had learned that there was no train for Geneva before the night-express. Lynde lighted the cigar which he had been unconsciously holding between his fingers all this while, and on the plea of cashing a draft at a banker's left the two gentlemen together. He wandered absently into the Place de la Concorde, crossed the crowded bridge there, and plunged into the narrow streets of the Latin Quarter. Finding his way back after an hour or so to the other bank of the Seine, he seated himself on one of those little black iron chairs which seem to have let themselves down like spiders from the lime-trees in the Champs Elysees, and remained for a long time in a deep study.

The meeting with Dr. Pendegrast had been so severe a shock to Lynde that he could not straightway recover his mental balance. The appalling shadow which the doctor's presence had for the moment thrown across him had left Lynde benumbed and chilled despite the reassuring sunshine of the doctor's words. By degrees, however, Lynde warmed to life again; his gloom slipped off and was lost in the restless tides of life which surged about him. It was the hour when Paris sits at small green tables in front of the cafes and sips its absinthe or cassis; when the boulevards are thronged, and the rich equipages come and go. There was not a cloud in the tender blue sky against which the reddish obelisk of Luxor looked like a column of jet; the fountains were playing in the Place de la Concorde, and in the Tuileries gardens beyond the breeze dreamily stirred the foliage which hid from Lynde's view the gray facade of the gutted palace, still standing there, calcined and cracked by the fires of the Commune. Presently all this began to distract him, and when he returned to the hotel he was in a humor that would have been comparatively tranquil if so many tedious miles had not stretched between Paris and Chamouni.

He found Mr. Denham and Dr. Pendegrast delaying dinner for him. After dinner, seeing no prospect of renewing conversation in private with the doctor, Lynde killed the time by writing a voluminous letter to Flemming, whose name he had stumbled on in the passenger-list of a steamer advertised to sail two days later from Liverpool.

As Lynde took his seat in the railroad carriage that night he had a feeling that several centuries had elapsed since daybreak. Every moment was a month to him until he could get back to Chamouni. The thought that Ruth might be dangerously ill scarcely presented itself among his reflections. She was free, he loved her, and there was no reason why he should not try to win her, however strongly the Denhams might be opposed to him. His mind was perfectly easy on that score; they had no right to wreck the girl's future in their shallow fear. His two travelling companions shortly dropped asleep, but Lynde did not close his eyes during those ten weary hours to Macon. Thence to Geneva was five hours more of impatience. At Geneva the party halted no longer than was necessary to refresh themselves at a buffet near the station and hire a conveyance to Chamouni, which they reached two or three hours after sunset. The town still lay, as Lynde had left it, in the portentous shadow of the mountain, with the sullen rain dropping from the black sky.

Lynde drew an alarming augury from the circumstance that Mrs. Denham did not come down to greet them. It dawned upon him then for the first time with any distinctness that Ruth might be fatally ill. Mr. Denham, accompanied by Dr. Pendegrast, hastened to his wife's apartments, and Lynde stationed himself at the head of a staircase in the hall, where he waited nearly an hour in intolerable suspense before the doctor reappeared.

"What is it, Doctor?"

"Pneumonia. No," he added, divining Lynde's unspoken thought even before it had fairly shaped itself in his brain, "it is not the other business."

"You are hiding the truth from me," said Lynde, with a pang. "She is dead!"

"No, but she is very low. The disease is approaching a crisis; a change must take place by to-morrow. Frankly, I dread that change. I am hiding nothing from you."

"Is there no hope? You do not mean that!"

"I am afraid I do. Perhaps it is because she is so dear to me that I always anticipate the worst when she is concerned. The other physician is more sanguine; but then he does not love Ruth as I do."

"You might have saved her!"

"Everything has been done that could be done. He is a person of remarkable skill, this Paris physician. I could have advised no change in his treatment of the case if I had been on the spot at first. That is a great deal for one physician to say of another. You had better go and get some rest," added Dr. Pendegrast in a changed voice, struck by the young man's ghastly look. "Your two night-journeys have used you up."

Lynde went mechanically to his room and threw himself upon the bed without undressing. He had no inclination to sleep, but his fatigue, bodily and mental, overcame him unawares as he lay listening to the wind which swept through the mountain-gorges, and rose and fell monotonously with a sound like the rote of the sea. It was a vision of the sea that filled his unrestful slumber: Ruth was dead, she had died in his arms, and he was standing woe-begone, like a ghost, on the deck of a homeward bound ship, with the gray, illimitable waste of waters stretching around him.

It appeared to Lynde to be in the middle of the night, though it was in fact on the edge of daybreak, that he was awakened by some one knocking softly at his door. He lighted a match, and by its momentary flicker saw Mr. Denham standing on the threshold.

"Ruth wishes to see you," he said indistinctly and with an indecisive air. "As nearly as we can gather, that is what she wants. Come quickly!"

Without waiting for a reply Mr. Denham turned and passed through the hall. Lynde followed in silence. He was less surprised than agitated by the summons; it was of a piece with the dream from which he had been roused.

There were candles burning on the mantel-piece of the chamber, and the dawn was whitening the window-panes. In that weird, blended light the face of the sick girl shone like a fading star. Lynde was conscious of no other presence, though Mrs. Denham and Dr. Pendegrast with a third person were standing near the chimney-place. Ruth raised her eyes and smiled upon Lynde as he came in; then her lids closed and did not open again, but the smile stayed in a dim way on her features, and a flush almost too faint to be perceived crept into her cheeks. Lynde stooped by the bed and took one of Ruth's hands. She turned her head slightly on the pillow, and after a moment her lips moved as if she were making an effort to speak. Lynde remained immobile, fearing to draw breath lest a word should escape his ear. But she did not speak. As he stood there listening in the breathless stillness, the flame of the candles burned fainter and fainter in the increasing daylight; a bird twittered somewhere aloft; then the sunshine streamed through the windows, and outside all the heights were touched with sudden gold.

[Illustration: But she did not speak]

Dr. Pendegrast approached Lynde and rested one finger on his arm. "You had better go now," the doctor whispered hastily. "I will come to you by and by."

Lynde was sitting on the side of the bed in his own room in the broad daylight. He had been sitting motionless in one posture for an hour—perhaps two hours, he could not tell how long—when Dr. Pendegrast opened the door without pausing to knock. Lynde felt the cold creeping about his heart.

"Doctor," he said desperately, "don't tell me!"

"Mr. Lynde," said Dr. Pendegrast, walking up to the bedside and speaking very slowly, as if he were doubtful of his own words and found it difficult to articulate them, "a change has taken place, but it is a change for the better. I believe that Ruth will live."

"She will live!"

"We thought she was sinking; she thought so herself, the poor child. You were worth a thousand doctors to her, that's my belief. Mrs. Denham was afraid to tell her you had gone to Paris to fetch us, thinking it would excite her. Ruth imagined that her aunt had offended you, and thought you had gone not to return."

"Ah!"

"That troubled her, in the state she was in—troubled her mightily. She has been able to take a few spoonfuls of nourishment," the doctor went on irrelevantly; "her pulse is improved; if she has no drawback she will get well."

Lynde looked around him bewilderedly for a moment; then he covered his face with his hands. "I thought she was dying!" he said under his breath.

That day and the next the girl's life hung by a thread; then the peril passed, and her recovery became merely a question of careful nursing. The days which immediately followed this certainty were the happiest Lynde had ever experienced. Perhaps it was because his chamber was directly over Ruth's that he sat there in the window-seat, reading from morning until night. It was as near to her as he was permitted to approach. He saw little of Mr. Denham and still less of Mrs. Denham during that week; but the doctor spent an hour or two every evening with Lynde, and did not find it tiresome to talk of nothing but his patient. The details of her convalescence were listened to with an interest that would have won Dr. Pendegrast if he had not already been very well disposed towards the young fellow, several of whose New York friends, as it transpired, were old acquaintances of the doctor's—Dr. Dillon and his family, and the Delaneys. The conversation between Lynde and Dr. Pendegrast at the Hotel Meurice had been hurried and disjointed, and in that respect unsatisfactory; but the minute history of Ruth's previous case, which the doctor related to Lynde in the course of those long summer nights, set his mind completely at rest.

"I could never have given her up, anyway," said Lynde to himself. "I have loved her for three years, though I didn't know it. That was my wife's slipper after all," he added, thinking of the time when it used to seem to be sitting up for him at night, on his writing-table at Rivermouth, and how often it threw a gloom over him with its tragic suggestion. "My wife's slipper!" He repeated the phrase softly to himself. There was nothing tragic in it now.

By and by the hours began to drag with him. The invalid could not get well fast enough to keep pace with his impatience. The day she was able for the first time to sit up a while, in an armchair wheeled by the bedside, was a fete day to the four Americans in the Couronne hotel. If Lynde did not exhaust his entire inheritance in cut flowers on this occasion, it was because Dr. Pendegrast objected to them in any profusion in a sick-chamber.

"When am I to see her?" asked Lynde that evening, as the doctor dropped into the room to make his usual report.

"Let me think. To-day is Tuesday—perhaps we shall let you see her by Friday or Saturday."

"Good heavens! why don't you put it off thirty or forty years?"

"I haven't the time," returned Dr. Pendegrast, laughing. "Seriously, she will not be strong enough until then to bear the least excitement. I am not going to run any risks with Ruth, I can tell you. You are very impatient, of course. I will give you a soothing draught."

"What is it?"

"A piece of information."

"I'll take it!"

"And a piece of advice."

"I'll take that, too; you can't frighten me."

"It is a betrayal of confidence on my part," said the doctor slowly, and with an air of reconsidering his offer.

"No matter."

"Well, then, Ruth's asking for you, the other night, rather amazed Denham when he came to think it over quietly, and Mrs. Denham judged it best to inform him of the conversation which took place between you and her the morning you set out for Paris. Denham was still more amazed. She had attempted to cure him of one astonishment by giving him another. Similia similibus curantur did not work that time. Then the two came to me for consultation, and I told them I thought Ruth's case required a doctor of divinity rather than a doctor of medicine."

"Did you say that!"

"Certainly I did. I strongly advised an operation, and designated the English church here as a proper place in which to have it performed. Moreover, as a change of air would be beneficial as soon as might be afterwards, I suggested for the invalid a short trip to Geneva—with not too much company. My dear fellow, you need not thank me; I am looking exclusively to Ruth's happiness—yours can come in incidentally, if it wants to. Mrs. Denham is YOUR ally."

"Is she, indeed? I thought differently. And Ruth"—

"Ruth," interposed the doctor, with a twinkle in his eyes, "Ruth is the good little girl in the primer who doesn't speak until she's spoken to."

"By Jove, she doesn't speak even then! I have tried her twice: once she evaded me, and once she refused to listen."

"The results of her false education," said the doctor sententiously.

Lynde laughed.

"To what view of the question does Mr. Denham incline?" he asked.

"Denham is not as unreasonable as he used to be; but he is somewhat stunned by the unexpectedness of the thing."

"That's the information; and now for the advice, Doctor."

"I advise you to speak with Denham the first chance you get. You will have an opportunity this evening. I took the liberty of asking him to come up here and smoke a cigar with us as soon as he finishes his coffee."

Lynde nodded his head approvingly, and the doctor went on—

"I shall leave you together after a while, and then you must manage it. At present he is in no state to deny Ruth anything; he would give her a lover just as he would buy her a pair of ear-rings. His joy over her escape from death—it was a fearfully narrow escape, let me tell you—has left him powerless. Moreover, her illness, in which there has not been a symptom of the old trouble, has reassured him on a most painful point. In short, everything is remarkably smooth for you. I think that's Denham's step now in the hall," added Dr. Pendegrast hurriedly. "You can say what you please to him of Ruth; but mind you, my dear boy, not a word at this juncture about the Queen of Sheba—she's dethroned, you know!"

XI

FROM CHAMOUNI TO GENEVA

One morning in September, a month after all this, three persons, a lady and two gentlemen, stood on the upper step of the Couronne hotel, waving farewell with their handkerchiefs to a carriage which had just started from the door and was gayly taking the road to St. Gervais-les-Bains, on the way to Geneva.

A cool purple light stretched along the valley and reached up the mountain side to where the eternal snows begin. The crown of Mont Blanc, muffled in its scarf of cloud, was invisible. The old monarch was in that disdainful mood which sometimes lasts him for months together. From those perilous heights came down a breath that chilled the air and tempered the sunshine falling upon Chamouni, now silent and deserted, for the season was well-nigh over. With the birds, their brothers, the summer tourists had flown southward at the rustling of the first autumnal leaf. Here and there a guide leaned idly against a post in front of one of the empty hotels. There was no other indication of life in the main street save the little group we have mentioned watching the departing carriage.

This carriage, a maroon body set upon red and black wheels, was drawn by four white horses and driven by the marquis. The doctor had prescribed white horses, and he took great credit to himself that morning as he stood on the hotel steps beside Mr. and Mrs. Denham, who followed the retreating vehicle rather thoughtfully with their eyes until it turned a corner of the narrow street and was lost to them.

As the horses slackened their speed at an ascending piece of ground outside the town, Lynde took Ruth's hand. The color of health had reasserted itself in her cheeks, but her eyes had not lost a certain depth of lustre which they had learned during her illness. The happy light in them illumined her face as she turned towards him.

"I don't believe a word of it!" cried Lynde. "It is just a dream, a cheating page out of a fairy-book. These horses are simply four white mice transformed. An hour ago, perhaps, this carriage was a pumpkin lying on the hearth of the hotel kitchen. The coachman is a good fairy in thin disguise of overcoat and false mustache. I am doubtful of even you. The whole thing is a delusion. It won't last, it can't last! Presently the wicked gnome that must needs dwell in a stalactite cavern somewhere hereabouts will start up and break the enchantment."

"It will never be broken so long as you love me," said Ruth softly. She smiled at Lynde's fancy, though his words had by no means badly expressed her own sense of doubt in respect to the reality of it all.

Here the driver leaned forward, skilfully touching the ear of the off-leader with the tip of his lash, and the carriage rolled away in the blue September weather. And here our story ends—at the very point, if we understand it, where life began for those two.

MY COUSIN THE COLONEL

I

Mrs. Wesley frequently embarrasses me by remarking in the presence of other persons—our intimate friends, of course—"Wesley, you are not brilliant, but you are good."

From Mrs. Wesley's outlook, which is that of a very high ideal, there is nothing uncomplimentary in the remark, nothing so intended, but I must confess that I have sometimes felt as if I were paying a rather large price for character. Yet when I reflect on my cousin the colonel, and my own action in the matter, I am ready with gratitude to accept Mrs. Wesley's estimate of me, for if I am not good, I am not anything. Perhaps it is an instance of my lack of brilliancy that I am willing to relate certain facts which strongly tend to substantiate this. My purpose, however, is not to prove either my goodness or my dulness, but to leave some record, even if slight and imperfect, of my only relative. When a family is reduced like ours to a single relative, it is well to make the most of him. One should celebrate him annually, as it were.

One morning in the latter part of May, a few weeks after the close of the war of the rebellion, as I was hurrying down Sixth Avenue in pursuit of a heedless horse-car, I ran against a young person whose shabbiness of aspect was all that impressed itself upon me in the instant of collision. At a second glance I saw that this person was clad in the uniform of a Confederate soldier—an officer's uniform originally, for there were signs that certain insignia of rank had been removed from the cuffs and collar of the threadbare coat. He wore a wide-brimmed felt hat of a military fashion, decorated with a tarnished gilt cord, the two ends of which, terminating in acorns, hung down over his nose. His butternut trousers were tucked into the tops of a pair of high cavalry boots, of such primitive workmanship as to suggest the possibility that the wearer had made them himself. In fact, his whole appearance had an impromptu air about it. The young man eyed me gloomily for half a minute; then a light came into his countenance.

"Wesley—Tom Wesley!" he exclaimed. "Dear old boy!"

To be sure I was Thomas Wesley, and, under conceivable circumstances, dear old boy; but who on earth was he?

"You don't know me?" he said, laying a hand on each of my shoulders, and leaning back as he contemplated me with a large smile in anticipatory enjoyment of my surprise and pleasure when I should come to know him. "I am George W. Flagg, and long may I wave!"

My cousin Flagg! It was no wonder that I did not recognize him.

When the Flagg family, consisting of father and son, removed to the South, George was ten years old and I was thirteen. It was twenty years since he and I had passed a few weeks together on grandfather Wesley's farm in New

Jersey. Our intimacy began and ended there, for it had not ripened into letters; perhaps because we were too young when we parted. Later I had had a hundred intermittent impulses to write to him, but did not. Meanwhile separation and silence had clothed him in my mind with something of the mistiness of a half-remembered dream. Yet the instant Washington Flagg mentioned his name the boyish features began rapidly to define themselves behind the maturer mask, until he stood before me in the crude form in which my memory had slyly embalmed him.

Now my sense of kinship is particularly strong, for reasons which I shall presently touch upon, and I straightway grasped my cousin's hand with a warmth that would have seemed exaggerated to a bystander, if there had been a bystander; but it was early in the day, and the avenue had not yet awakened to life. As this bitter world goes, a sleek, prosperous, well-dressed man does not usually throw much heartiness into his manner when he is accosted on the street by so unpromising and dismal an object as my cousin Washington Flagg was that morning. Not at all in the way of sounding the trumpet of my own geniality, but simply as the statement of a fact, I will say that I threw a great deal of heartiness into my greeting. This man to me meant Family.

I stood curiously alone in the world. My father died before I was born, and my mother shortly afterwards. I had neither brother nor sister. Indeed, I never had any near relatives except a grandfather until my sons came along. Mrs. Wesley, when I married her, was not merely an only child, but an orphan. Fate denied me even a mother-in-law. I had one uncle and one cousin. The former I do not remember ever to have seen, and my association with the latter, as has been stated, was of a most limited order. Perhaps I should have had less sentiment about family ties if I had had more of them. As it was, Washington Flagg occupied the position of sole kinsman, always excepting the little Wesleys, and I was as glad to see him that May morning in his poverty as if he had come to me loaded with the title-deeds of those vast estates which our ancestors (I wonder that I was allowed any ancestors: why wasn't I created at once out of some stray scrap of protoplasm?) were supposed to have held in the colonial period. As I gazed upon Washington Flagg I thrilled with the sense that I was gazing upon the materialization in a concrete form of all the ghostly brothers and sisters and nephews and nieces which I had never had.

"Dear old boy!" I exclaimed, in my turn, holding on to his hand as if I were afraid that I was going to lose him again for another twenty years. "Bless my stars! where did you come from?"

"From Dixie's Land," he said, with a laugh. "'Way down in Dixie."

In a few words, and with a picturesqueness of phrase in which I noted a rich Southern flavor, he explained the phenomenon of his presence in New York. After Lee's surrender at Appomattox Court-House, my cousin had managed to reach Washington, where he was fortunate enough to get a free pass to Baltimore. He had nearly starved to death in making his way out of Virginia. To quote his words, "The wind that is supposed to be tempered expressly for shorn lambs was not blowing very heavily about that time." At Baltimore he fell in with a former Mobile acquaintance, from whom he borrowed a sum sufficient to pay the fare to New York—a humiliating necessity, as my cousin remarked, for a man who had been a colonel in Stonewall Jackson's brigade. Flagg had reached the city before daybreak, and had wandered for hours along the water-front, waiting for some place to open, in order that he might look up my address in the Directory, if I were still in the land of the living. He had had what he described as an antediluvian sandwich the previous day at two o'clock, since which banquet no food had passed his lips.

"And I'll be hanged," he said, "if the first shop that took down its shutters wasn't a restaurant, with a cursed rib of roast beef, flanked with celery, and a ham in curl-papers staring at me through the window-pane. A little tin sign, with 'Meals at All Hours' painted on it—what did they want to go and do that for?—knocked the breath clean out of me. I gave one look, and ploughed up the street, for if I had stayed fifteen seconds longer in front of that plate-glass, I reckon I would have burst it in. Well, I put distance between me and temptation, and by and by I came to a newspaper office, where I cornered a Directory. I was on the way to your house when we collided; and now, Tom Wesley, for heaven's sake introduce me to something to eat. There is no false pride about me; I'd shake hands with a bone."

The moisture was ready to gather in my eyes, and for a second or two I was unable to manage my voice. Here was my only kinsman on the verge of collapse—one miserable sandwich, like a thin plank, between him and destruction. My own plenteous though hasty morning meal turned into reproachful lead within me.

"Dear old boy!" I cried again. "Come along! I can see that you are nearly famished."

"I've a right smart appetite, Thomas, there's no mistake about that. If appetite were assets, I could invite a whole regiment to rations."

I had thrust my hand under his arm, and was dragging him towards a small oyster shop, whose red balloon in a side street had caught my eye, when I suddenly remembered that it was imperative on me to be at the office at eight o'clock that morning, in order to prepare certain papers wanted by the president of the board, previous to a meeting of the directors. (I was at that time under-secretary of the Savonarola Fire Insurance Company.) The recollection of the business which had caused me to be on foot at this unusual hour brought me to a dead halt. I dropped my cousin's arm, and stood looking at him helplessly. It seemed so inhospitable, not to say cold-blooded, to send him off to get his breakfast alone. Flagg misinterpreted my embarrassment.

"Of course," he said, with a touch of dignity which pierced me through the bosom, "I do not wish to be taken to any place where I would disgrace you. I know how impossible I am. Yet this suit of clothes cost me twelve hundred dollars in Confederate scrip. These boots are not much to look at, but they were made by a scion of one of the first families of the South; I paid him two hundred dollars for them, and he was right glad to get it. To such miserable straits have Southern gentlemen been reduced by the vandals of the North. Perhaps you don't like the Confederate gray?"

"Bother your boots and your clothes!" I cried. "Nobody will notice them here." (Which was true enough, for in those days the land was strewed with shreds and patches of the war. The drivers and conductors of street cars wore overcoats made out of shoddy army blankets, and the dustmen went about in cast-off infantry caps.) "What troubles me is that I can't wait to start you on your breakfast."

"I reckon I don't need much starting."

I explained the situation to him, and suggested that instead of going to the restaurant, he should go directly to my house, and be served by Mrs. Wesley, to whom I would write a line on a leaf of my memorandum-book. I did not suggest this step in the first instance because the little oyster saloon, close at hand, had seemed to offer the shortest cut to my cousin's relief.

"So you're married?" said he.

"Yes—and you?"

"I haven't taken any matrimony in mine."

"I've been married six years, and have two boys."

"No! How far is your house?" he inquired. "Will I have to take a caar?"

"A 'caar'? Ah, yes—that is to say, no. A car isn't worth while. You see that bakery two blocks from here, at the right? That's on the corner of Clinton Place. You turn down there. You'll notice in looking over what I've written to Mrs. Wesley that she is to furnish you with some clothes, such as are worn by—by vandals of the North in comfortable circumstances."

"Tom Wesley, you are as good as a straight flush. If you ever come down South, when this cruel war is over, our people will treat you like one of the crowned heads—only a devilish sight better, for the crowned heads rather went back on us. If England had recognized the Southern Confederacy"—

"Never mind that; your tenderloin steak is cooling."

"Don't mention it! I go. But I say, Tom—Mrs. Wesley? Really, I am hardly presentable. Are there other ladies around?"

"There's no one but Mrs. Wesley."

"Do you think I can count on her being glad to see me at such short notice?"

"She will be a sister to you," I said warmly.

"Well, I reckon that you two are a pair of trumps. Au revoir! Be good to yourself."

With this, my cousin strode off, tucking my note to Mrs. Wesley inside the leather belt buckled tightly around his waist. I lingered a moment on the curbstone, and looked after him with a sensation of mingled pride, amusement, and curiosity. That was my Family; there it was, in that broad back and those not ungraceful legs, striding up Sixth Avenue, with its noble intellect intent on thoughts of breakfast. I was thankful that it had not been written in the book of fate that this limb of the closely pruned Wesley tree should be lopped off by the sword of war. But as Washington Flagg turned into Clinton Place, I had a misgiving. It was hardly to be expected that a person of his temperament, fresh from a four years' desperate struggle and a disastrous defeat, would refrain from expressing his views on the subject. That those views would be somewhat lurid, I was convinced by the phrases which he had dropped here and there in the course of our conversation. He was, to all intents and purposes, a Southerner. He had been a colonel in Stonewall Jackson's brigade. And Mrs. Wesley was such an uncompromising patriot! It was in the blood. Her great-grandfather, on the mother's side, had frozen to death at Valley Forge in the winter of 1778, and her grandfather, on the paternal side, had had his head taken off by a round-shot from his Majesty's sloop of war Porpoise in 1812. I believe that Mrs. Wesley would have applied for a divorce from me if I had not served a year in the army at the beginning of the war.

I began bitterly to regret that I had been obliged to present my cousin to her so abruptly. I wished it had occurred to me to give him a word or two of caution, or that I had had sense enough to adhere to my first plan of letting him feed himself at the little oyster establishment round the corner. But wishes and regrets could not now mend the matter; so I hailed an approaching horse-car, and comforted myself on the rear platform with the reflection that perhaps the colonel would not wave the palmetto leaf too vigorously, if he waved it at all, in the face of Mrs. Wesley.

II

The awkwardness of the situation disturbed me more or less during the forenoon; but fortunately it was a half-holiday, and I was able to leave the office shortly after one o'clock.

I do not know how I came to work myself into such a state of mind on the way up town, but as I stepped from the horse-car and turned into Clinton Place I had a strong apprehension that I should find some unpleasant change in the facial aspect of the little red brick building I occupied—a scowl, for instance, on the brown-stone eyebrow over the front door. I actually had a feeling of relief when I saw that the facade presented its usual unaggressive appearance.

As I entered the hall, Mrs. Wesley, who had heard my pass-key grating in the lock, was coming down-stairs.

"Is my cousin here, Clara?" I asked, in the act of reaching up to hang my hat on the rack.

"No," said Mrs. Wesley. There was a tone in that monosyllable that struck me. "But he has been here?"

"He has been here," replied Mrs. Wesley. "May be you noticed the bell-knob hanging out one or two inches. Is Mr. Flagg in the habit of stretching the bell-wire of the houses he visits, when the door is not opened in a moment? Has he escaped from somewhere?"

"Escaped from somewhere!" I echoed. "I only asked; he behaved so strangely."

"Good heavens, Clara! what has the man done? I hope that nothing unpleasant has happened. Flagg is my only surviving relative—I may say our only surviving relative—and I should be pained to have any misunderstanding. I want you to like him."

"There was a slight misunderstanding at first," said Clara, and a smile flitted across her face, softening the features which had worn an air of unusual seriousness and preoccupation. "But it is all right now, dear. He has eaten everything in the house—that bit of spring lamb I saved expressly for you!— and has gone down town 'on a raid,' as he called it, in your second-best suit— the checked tweed. I did all I could for him."

"My dear, something has ruffled you. What is it?"

"Wesley," said my wife slowly, and in a perplexed way, "I have had so few relatives that perhaps I don't know what to do with them, or what to say to them."

"You always say and do what is just right."

"I began unfortunately with Mr. Flagg, then. Mary was washing the dishes when he rang, and I went to the door. If he IS our cousin, I must say that he cut a remarkable figure on the doorstep."

"I can imagine it, my dear, coming upon you so unexpectedly. There were peculiarities in his costume."

"For an instant," Clara went on, "I took him for the ashman, though the ashman always goes to the area door, and never comes on Tuesdays; and then, before the creature had a chance to speak, I said, 'We don't want any,' supposing he had something to sell. Instead of going away quietly, as I expected he would do, the man made a motion to come in, and I slammed the door on him."

"Dear! dear!"

"What else could I do, all alone in the hall? How was I to know that he was one of the family?"

"What happened next?"

"Well, I saw that I had shut the lapel of his coat in the door-jamb, and that the man couldn't go away if he wanted to ever so much. Wasn't it dreadful? Of course I didn't dare to open the door, and there he was! He began pounding on the panels and ringing the bell in a manner to curdle one's blood. He rang the bell at least a hundred times in succession. I stood there with my hand on the bolt, not daring to move or breathe. I called to Mary to put on her things, steal out the lower way, and bring the police. Suddenly everything was still outside, and presently I saw a piece of paper slowly slipping in over the threshold, oh, so slyly! I felt my hands and feet grow cold. I felt that the man himself was about to follow that narrow strip of paper; that he was bound to get in that way, or through the keyhole, or somehow. Then I recognized your handwriting. My first thought was that you had been killed in some horrible accident"—

"And had dropped you a line?"

"I didn't reason about it, Wesley; I was paralyzed. I picked up the paper, and read it, and opened the door, and Mr. Flagg rushed in as if he had been shot out of something. 'Don't want any?' he shouted. 'But I do! I want some breakfast!' You should have heard him."

"He stated a fact, at any rate. To be sure he might have stated it less vivaciously." I was beginning to be amused.

"After that he was quieter, and tried to make himself agreeable, and we laughed a little together over my mistake—that is, HE laughed. Of course I got breakfast for him—and such a breakfast!"

"He had been without anything to eat since yesterday."

"I should have imagined," said Clara, "that he had eaten nothing since the war broke out."

"Did he say anything in particular about himself?" I asked, with a recurrent touch of anxiety.

"He wasn't particular what he said about himself. Without in the least seeing the horror of it, he positively boasted of having been in the rebel army."

"Yes—a colonel."

"That makes it all the worse," replied Clara.

"But they had to have colonels, you know."

"Is Mr. Flagg a Virginian, or a Mississippian, or a Georgian?"

"No, my dear; he was born in the State of Maine; but he has lived so long in the South that he's quite one of them for the present. We must make allowances for him, Clara. Did he say anything else?"

"Oh, yes."

"What did he say?"

"He said he'd come back to supper."

It was clear that Clara was not favorably impressed by my cousin, and, indeed, the circumstances attending his advent were not happy. It was likewise clear that I had him on my hands, temporarily at least. I almost reproach myself even now for saying "on my hands," in connection with my own flesh and blood. The responsibility did not so define itself at the time. It took the form of a novel and pleasing duty. Here was my only kinsman, in a strange city, without friends, money, or hopeful outlook. My course lay before me as straight as a turnpike. I had a great deal of family pride, even if I did not have any family to speak of, and I was resolved that what little I had should not perish for want of proper sustenance.

Shortly before six o'clock Washington Flagg again presented himself at our doorstep, and obtained admission to the house with fewer difficulties than he had encountered earlier in the day.

I do not think I ever saw a man in destitute circumstances so entirely cheerful as my cousin was. Neither the immediate past, which must have been full of hardships, nor the immediate future, which was not lavish of its promises, seemed to give him any but a momentary and impersonal concern. At the supper-table he talked much and well, exceedingly well, I thought, except when he touched on the war, which he was continually doing, and then I was on tenter-hooks. His point of view was so opposed to ours as to threaten in several instances to bring on an engagement all along the line. This calamity was averted by my passing something to him at the critical moment. Now I checked his advance by a slice of cold tongue, and now I turned his flank with another cup of tea; but I questioned my ability to preserve peace throughout the evening. Before the meal was at an end there had crept into Clara's manner a polite calmness which I never liked to see. What was I going to do with these two after supper, when my cousin Flagg, with his mind undistracted by relays of cream toast, could give his entire attention to the Lost Cause?

As we were pushing the chairs back from the table, I was inspired with the idea of taking our guest off to a cafe concert over in the Bowery—a volksgarten very popular in those days. While my whispered suggestion was meeting Clara's cordial approval, our friend Bleeker dropped in. So the colonel and Bleeker and I passed the evening with "lager-beer and Meyer-beer," as my lively kinsman put it; after which he spent the night on the sofa in our sitting-room, for we had no spare chamber to place at his disposal.

"I shall be very snug here," he said, smiling down my apologies. "I'm a 'possum for adapting myself to any odd hollow."

The next morning my cousin was early astir, possibly not having found that narrow springless lounge all a 'possum could wish, and joined us in discussing a plan which I had proposed overnight to Mrs. Wesley, namely, that he should hire an apartment in a quiet street near by, and take his meals—that was to say, his dinner—with us, until he could make such arrangements as would allow him to live more conveniently. To return South, where all the lines of his previous business connections were presumably broken, was at present out of the question.

"The war has ruined our people," said the colonel. "I will have to put up for a while with a place in a bank or an insurance office, or something in that small way. The world owes me a living, North or South."

His remark nettled me a little, though he was, of course, unaware of my relations with the Savonarola Fire Insurance Company, and had meant no slight.

"I don't quite see that," I observed.

"Don't see what?"

"How the world contrived to get so deeply into your debt—how all the points of the compass managed it."

"Thomas, I didn't ask to be born, did I?"

"Probably not."

"But I was born, wasn't I?"

"To all appearances."

"Well, then!"

"But you cannot hold the world in general responsible for your birth. The responsibility narrows itself down to your parents."

"Then I am euchred. By one of those laws of nature which make this globe a sweet spot to live on, they were taken from me just when I needed them most— my mother in my infancy, and my father in my childhood."

"But your father left you something?"

"The old gentleman left me nothing, and I've been steadily increasing the legacy ever since."

"What did you do before the war?" inquired Clara sympathetically. His mention of his early losses had touched her.

"Oh, a number of things. I read law for a while. At one time I was interested in a large concern for the manufacture of patent metallic burial cases; but nobody seemed to die that year. Good health raged like an epidemic all over the South. Latterly I dabbled a little in stocks—and stocks dabbled in me."

"You were not successful, then?" I said.

"I was at first, but when the war fever broke out and the Southern heart was fired, everything that didn't go down went up."

"And you couldn't meet your obligations?"

"That wasn't the trouble—I couldn't get away from them," replied the colonel, with a winsome smile. "I met them at every corner."

The man had a fashion of turning his very misfortunes into pleasantries. Surely prosperity would be wasted on a person so gifted with optimism. I felt it to be kind and proper, however, to express the hope that he had reached the end of his adversity, and to assure him that I would do anything I could in the world to help him.

"Tom Wesley, I believe you would."

Before the close of that day Mrs. Wesley, who is a lady that does not allow any species of vegetation to accumulate under her feet, had secured a furnished room for our kinsman in a street branching off from Clinton Place, and at a moderate additional expense contracted to have him served with breakfast on the premises. Previous to this I had dined down town, returning home in the evening to a rather heavy tea, which was really my wife's dinner—Sheridan and Ulysses (such were the heroic names under which the two little Wesleys were staggering) had their principal meal at midday. It was, of course, not desirable that the colonel should share this meal with them and Mrs. Wesley in my absence. So we decided to have a six o'clock dinner; a temporary disarrangement of our domestic machinery, for my cousin Flagg would doubtless find some acceptable employment before long, and leave the household free to slip back into its regular grooves.

An outline of the physical aspects of the exotic kinsman who had so unexpectedly added himself to the figures at our happy fireside seems not out of place here. The portrait, being the result of many sittings, does not in some points convey the exact impression he made upon us in the earlier moments of our intimacy; but that is not important.

Though Washington Flagg had first opened his eyes on the banks of the Penobscot, he appeared to have been planned by nature to adorn the banks of the Rappahannock. There was nothing of the New Englander about him. The sallowness of his complexion and the blackness of his straight hair, which he wore long, were those of the typical Southerner. He was of medium height and loosely built, with a kind of elastic grace in his disjointedness. When he smiled he was positively handsome; in repose his features were nearly plain, the lips too indecisive, and the eyes lacking in lustre. A sparse tuft of beard at his chin—he was otherwise smoothly shaven—lengthened the face. There was, when he willed it, something very ingratiating in his manner—even Clara admitted that—a courteous and unconventional sort of ease. In all these surface characteristics he was a geographical anomaly. In the cast of his mind he was more Southern than the South, as a Northern convert is apt to be. Even his speech, like the dyer's arm, had taken tints from his environment. One might say that his pronunciation had literally been colored by his long association with the colored race. He invariably said flo' for floor, and djew for dew; but I do not anywhere attempt a phonetic reproduction of his dialect; in its finer qualities it was too elusive to be snared in a network of letters. In spite of his displacements, for my cousin had lived all over the South in his boyhood, he had contrived to pick up a very decent education. As to his other attributes, he shall be left to reveal them himself.

Mrs. Wesley kindly assumed the charge of establishing Washington Flagg in his headquarters, as he termed the snug hall bedroom in Macdougal Street. There were numberless details to be looked to. His wardrobe, among the rest, needed replenishing down to the most unconsidered button, for Flagg had dropped into our little world with as few impedimenta as if he had been a newly born infant. Though my condition, like that desired by Agur, the son of Jakeh, was one of neither poverty nor riches, greenbacks in those days were greenbacks. I mention the fact in order to say that my satisfaction in coming to the rescue of my kinsman would have been greatly lessened if it had involved no self-denial whatever.

The day following his installation I was partly annoyed, partly amused, to find that Flagg had purchased a rather expensive meerschaum pipe and a pound or two of Latakia tobacco.

"I cannot afford to smoke cigars," he explained. "I must economize until I get on my feet."

Perhaps it would have been wiser if I had personally attended to his expenditures, minor as well as major, but it did not seem practicable to leave him without a cent in his pocket. His pilgrimage down town that forenoon had apparently had no purpose beyond this purchase, though on the previous evening I had directed his notice to two or three commercial advertisements which impressed me as worth looking into. I hesitated to ask him if he had looked into them. A collateral feeling of delicacy prevented me from breathing a word to Clara about the pipe.

Our reconstructed household, with its unreconstructed member, now moved forward on the lines laid down. Punctually at a quarter to six P. M. my cousin appeared at the front door, hung his hat on the rack, and passed into the sitting-room, sometimes humming in the hall a bar or two of The Bonny Blue Flag that bears a Single Star, to the infinite distaste of Mrs. Wesley, who was usually at that moment giving the finishing touches to the dinner-table. After dinner, during which I was in a state of unrelaxed anxiety lest the colonel should get himself on too delicate ground, I took him into my small snuggery at the foot of the hall, where coffee was served to us, Mrs. Wesley being left to her own devices.

For several days matters went as smoothly as I could have hoped. I found it so easy, when desirable, to switch the colonel on to one of my carefully contrived side tracks that I began to be proud of my skill and to enjoy the exercise of it. But one evening, just as we were in the middle of the dessert, he suddenly broke out with, "We were conquered by mere brute force, you know!"

"That is very true," I replied. "It is brute force that tells in war. Wasn't it Napoleon who said that he had remarked that God was generally on the side which had the heaviest artillery?"

"The North had that, fast enough, and crushed a free people with it."

"A free people with four millions of slaves?" observed Mrs. Wesley quietly.

"Slavery was a patriarchal institution, my dear lady. But I reckon it is exploded now. The Emancipation Proclamation was a dastardly war measure."

"It did something more and better than free the blacks," said Mrs. Wesley; "it freed the whites. Dear me!" she added, glancing at Sheridan and Ulysses, who, in a brief reprieve from bed, were over in one corner of the room dissecting a small wooden camel, "I cannot be thankful enough that the children are too young to understand such sentiments."

The colonel, to my great relief, remained silent; but as soon as Clara had closed the dining-room door behind her, he said, "Tom Wesley, I reckon your wife doesn't wholly like me."

"She likes you immensely," I cried, inwardly begging to be forgiven. "But she is a firm believer in the justice of the Northern cause."

"May be she lost a brother, or something."

"No; she never had a brother. If she had had one, he would have been killed in the first battle of the war. She sent me to the front to be killed, and I went willingly; but I wasn't good enough; the enemy wouldn't have me at any price after a year's trial. Mrs. Wesley feels very strongly on this subject, and I wish you would try, like a good fellow, not to bring the question up at dinner-time. I am squarely opposed to your views myself, but I don't mind what you say as she does. So talk to me as much as you want to, but don't talk in Clara's presence. When persons disagree as you two do, argument is useless. Besides, the whole thing has been settled on the battlefield, and it isn't worth while to fight it all over again on a table-cloth."

"I suppose it isn't," he assented good-naturedly. "But you people up at the North here don't suspicion what we have been through. You caught only the edge of the hurricane. The most of you, I take it, weren't in it at all."

"Our dearest were in it."

"Well, we got whipped, Wesley, I acknowledge it; but we deserved to win, if ever bravery deserved it."

"The South was brave, nobody contests that; but 't is not enough to be brave'—

"'The angry valor dashed. On the awful shield of God,'

As one of our poets says."

"Blast one of your poets! Our people were right, too."

"Come, now, Flagg, when you talk about your people, you ought to mean Northerners, for you were born in the North."

"That was just the kind of luck that has followed me all my life. My body belongs to Bangor, Maine, and my soul to Charleston, South Carolina."

"You've got a problem there that ought to bother you."

"It does," said the colonel, with a laugh.

"Meanwhile, my dear boy, don't distress Mrs. Wesley with it. She is ready to be very fond of you, if you will let her. It would be altogether sad and shameful if a family so contracted as ours couldn't get along without internal dissensions."

My cousin instantly professed the greatest regard for Mrs. Wesley, and declared that both of us were good enough to be Southrons. He promised that in future he would take all the care he could not to run against her prejudices, which merely grew out of her confused conception of State rights and the right of self-government. Women never understood anything about political economy and government, anyhow.

Having accomplished thus much with the colonel, I turned my attention, on his departure, to smoothing Clara. I reminded her that nearly everybody North and South had kinsmen or friends in both armies. To be sure, it was unfortunate that we, having only one kinsman, should have had him on the wrong side. That was better than having no kinsman at all. (Clara was inclined to demur at this.) It had not been practicable for him to divide himself; if it had been, he would probably have done it, and the two halves would doubtless have arrayed themselves against each other. They would, in a manner, have been bound to do so. However, the war was over, we were victorious, and could afford to be magnanimous.

"But he doesn't seem to have discovered that the war is over," returned Clara. "He 'still waves.'"

"It is likely that certain obstinate persons on both sides of Mason and Dixon's line will be a long time making the discovery. Some will never make it—so much the worse for them and the country."

Mrs. Wesley meditated and said nothing, but I saw that so far as she and the colonel were concerned the war was not over.

IV

This slight breeze cleared the atmosphere for the time being. My cousin Flagg took pains to avoid all but the most indirect allusions to the war, except when we were alone, and in several small ways endeavored—with not too dazzling success—to be agreeable to Clara. The transparency of the effort was perhaps the partial cause of its failure. And then, too, the nature of his little attentions was not always carefully considered on his part. For example, Mrs. Wesley could hardly be expected to lend herself with any grace at all to the proposal he made one sultry June evening to "knock her up" a mint-julep, "the most refreshing beverage on earth, madam, in hot weather, I can assure you." Judge Ashburton Todhunter, of Fauquier County, had taught him to prepare this pungent elixir from a private receipt for which the judge had once refused the sum of fifty dollars, offered to him by Colonel Stanley Bluegrass, of Chattanooga, and this was at a moment, too, when the judge had been losing very heavily at draw poker.

"All quiet along the Potomac," whispered the colonel, with a momentary pride in the pacific relations he had established between himself and Mrs. Wesley.

As the mint and one or two other necessary ingredients were lacking to our family stores, the idea of julep was dismissed as a vain dream, and its place supplied by iced Congress water, a liquid which my cousin characterized, in a hasty aside to me, as being a drink fit only for imbecile infants of a tender age.

Washington Flagg's frequent and familiar mention of governors, judges, colonels, and majors clearly indicated that he had moved in aristocratic latitudes in the South, and threw light on his disinclination to consider any of the humbler employments which might have been open to him. He had so far conceded to the exigency of the case as to inquire if there were a possible chance for him in the Savonarola Fire Insurance Company. He had learned of my secretaryship. There was no vacancy in the office, and if there had been, I would have taken no steps to fill it with my cousin. He knew nothing of the business. Besides, however deeply I had his interests at heart, I should have hesitated to risk my own situation by becoming sponsor for so unmanageable an element as he appeared to be.

At odd times in my snuggery after dinner Flagg glanced over the "wants" columns of the evening journal, but never found anything he wanted. He found many amusing advertisements that served him as pegs on which to hang witty comment, but nothing to be taken seriously. I ventured to suggest that he should advertise. He received the idea with little warmth.

"No, my dear boy, I can't join the long procession of scullions, cooks, butlers, valets, and bottle-washers which seem to make up so large a part of your population. I couldn't keep step with them. It is altogether impossible for me to conduct myself in this matter like a menial-of-all-work out of place. 'Wanted, a situation, by a respectable young person of temperate habits;

understands the care of horses; is willing to go into the country and milk the cow with the crumpled horn.' No; many thanks."

"State your own requirements, Flagg. I didn't propose that you should offer yourself as coachman."

"It would amount to the same thing, Wesley. I should at once be relegated to his level. Some large opportunity is dead sure to present itself to me if I wait. I believe the office should seek the man."

"I have noticed that a man has to meet his opportunities more than halfway, or he doesn't get acquainted with them. Mohammed was obliged to go to the mountain, after waiting for the mountain to come to him."

"Mohammed's mistake was that he didn't wait long enough. He was too impatient. But don't you fret. I have come to Yankeedom to make my fortune. The despot's heel is on your shore, and it means to remain there until he hears of something greatly to his advantage."

A few days following this conversation, Mr. Nelson, of Files & Nelson, wholesale grocers on Front Street, mentioned to me casually that he was looking for a shipping-clerk. Before the war the firm had done an extensive Southern trade, which they purposed to build up again now that the ports of the South were thrown open. The place in question involved a great deal of outdoor work—the loading and unloading of spicy cargoes, a life among the piers—all which seemed to me just suited to my cousin's woodland nature. I could not picture him nailed to a desk in a counting-room. The salary was not bewildering, but the sum was to be elastic, if ability were shown. Here was an excellent chance, a stepping-stone, at all events; perhaps the large opportunity itself, artfully disguised as fifteen dollars a week. I spoke of Flagg to Mr. Nelson, and arranged a meeting between them for the next day.

I said nothing of the matter at the dinner-table that evening; but an encouraging thing always makes a lantern of me, and Clara saw the light in my face. As soon as dinner was over I drew my cousin into the little side room, and laid the affair before him.

"And I have made an appointment for you to meet Mr. Nelson to-morrow at one o'clock," I said, in conclusion.

"My dear Wesley"—he had listened to me in silence, and now spoke without enthusiasm—"I don't know what you were thinking of to do anything of the sort. I will not keep the appointment with that person. The only possible intercourse I could have with him would be to order groceries at his shop. The idea of a man who has moved in the best society of the South, who has been engaged in great if unsuccessful enterprises, who has led the picked chivalry of his oppressed land against the Northern hordes—the idea of a gentleman of this kidney meekly simmering down into a factotum to a Yankee dealer in canned goods! No, sir; I reckon I can do better than that."

The lantern went out.

I resolved that moment to let my cousin shape his own destiny—a task which in no way appeared to trouble him. And, indeed, now that I look back to it, why should he have troubled himself? He had a comfortable if not luxurious apartment in Macdougal Street; a daily dinner that asked only to be eaten; a wardrobe that was replenished when it needed replenishing; a weekly allowance that made up for its modesty by its punctuality. If ever a man was in a position patiently to await the obsequious approach of large opportunities that man was Washington Flagg. He was not insensible to the fact. He passed his time serenely. He walked the streets—Flagg was a great walker—sometimes wandering for hours in the Central Park. His Southern life, passed partly among plantations, had given him a relish for trees and rocks and waters. He was also a hungry reader of novels. When he had devoured our slender store of fiction, which was soon done, he took books from a small circulating library on Sixth Avenue. That he gave no thought whatever to the future was clear. He simply drifted down the gentle stream of the present. Sufficient to the day was the sunshine thereof.

In spite of his unforgivable inertia, and the egotism that enveloped him like an atmosphere, there was a charm to the man that put my impatience to sleep. I tried to think that this indifference and sunny idleness were perhaps the natural reaction of that larger life of emotion and activity from which he had just emerged. I reflected a great deal on that life, and, though I lamented the fact that he had drawn his sword on the wrong side, there was, down deep in my heart, an involuntary sympathetic throb for the valor that had not availed. I suppose the inexplicable ties of kinship had something to do with all this.

Washington Flagg had now been with us five weeks. He usually lingered awhile after dinner; sometimes spent the entire evening with the family, or, rather, with me, for Mrs. Wesley preferred the sitting-room to my den when I had company. Besides, there were Sheridan and Ulysses to be looked to. Toward the close of the sixth week I noticed that Flagg had fallen into a way of leaving immediately after dinner. He had also fallen into another way not so open to pleasant criticism.

By degrees—by degrees so subtle as almost to escape measurement—he had glided back to the forbidden and dangerous ground of the war. At first it was an intangible reference to something that occurred on such and such a date, the date in question being that of some sanguinary battle; then a swift sarcasm, veiled and softly shod; then a sarcasm that dropped its veil for an instant, and showed its sharp features. At last his thought wore no disguise. Possibly the man could not help it; possibly there was something in the atmosphere of the house that impelled him to say things which he would have been unlikely to say elsewhere. Whatever was the explanation, my cousin Flagg began to make himself disagreeable again at meal-times.

He had never much regarded my disapproval, and now his early ill-defined fear of Mrs. Wesley was evaporated. He no longer hesitated to indulge in his war reminiscences, which necessarily brought his personal exploits under a calcium-light. These exploits usually emphasized his intimacy with some of the more dashing Southern leaders, such as Stonewall Jackson and Jeb Stuart and Mosby. We found ourselves practically conscripted in the Confederate army. We were taken on long midnight rides through the passes of the Cumberland Mountains and hurled on some Federal outpost; we were made—a mere handful as we were—to assault and carry most formidable earthworks; we crossed dangerous fords, and bivouacked under boughs hung with weird gonfalons of gray moss, slit here and there by the edge of a star. Many a time we crawled stealthily through tangled vines and shrubs to the skirt of a wood, and across a fallen log sighted the Yankee picket whose bayonet point glimmered now and then far off in the moonlight. We spent a great many hours around the camp-fire counting our metaphorical scalps.

One evening the colonel was especially exasperating with anecdotes of Stonewall Jackson, and details of what he said to the general and what the general said to him.

"Stonewall Jackson often used to say to me, 'George'—he always called me George, in just that off-hand way—'George, when we get to New York, you shall have quarters in the Astor House, and pasture your mare Spitfire in the Park.'"

"That was very thoughtful of Stonewall Jackson," remarked Mrs. Wesley, with the faintest little whiteness gathering at the lips. "I am sorry that your late friend did not accompany you to the city, and personally superintend your settlement here. He would have been able to surround you with so many more comforts than you have in Macdougal Street."

The colonel smiled upon Clara, and made a deprecating gesture with his left hand. Nothing seemed to pierce his ironclad composure. A moment afterward he returned to the theme, and recited some verses called "Stonewall Jackson's Way." He recited them very well. One stanza lingers in my memory—

> "We see him now—the old slouched hat
> Cocked o'er his brow askew,
> The shrewd, dry smile, the speech so pat,
> So calm, so blunt, so true.
> The Blue-light Elder knows 'em well.
> Says he: 'That's Banks; he's fond of shell.
> Lord save his soul! we'll give him'—Well,
> That's Stonewall Jackson's way."

"His ways must have been far from agreeable," observed my wife, "if that is a sample of them."

After the colonel had taken himself off, Mrs. Wesley, sinking wearily upon the sofa, said, "I think I am getting rather tired of Stonewall Jackson."

"We both are, my dear; and some of our corps commanders used to find him rather tiresome now and then. He was really a great soldier, Clara; perhaps the greatest on the other side."

"I suppose he was; but Flagg comes next—according to his own report. Why, Tom, if your cousin had been in all the battles he says he has, the man would have been killed ten times over. He'd have had at least an arm or a leg shot off."

That Washington Flagg had all his limbs on was actually becoming a grievance to Mrs. Wesley.

The situation filled me with anxiety. Between my cousin's deplorable attitude and my wife's justifiable irritation, I was extremely perplexed. If I had had a dozen cousins, the solution of the difficulty would have been simple. But to close our door on our only kinsman was an intolerable alternative.

If any word of mine has caused the impression that Clara was not gentle and sympathetic and altogether feminine, I have wronged her. The reserve which strangers mistook for coldness was a shell that melted at the slightest kind touch, her masterful air the merest seeming. But whatever latent antagonism lay in her nature the colonel had the faculty of bringing to the surface. It must be conceded that the circumstances in which she was placed were trying, and Clara was without that strong, perhaps abnormal, sense of relationship which sustained me in the ordeal. Later on, when matters grew more complicated, I could but admire her resignation—if it were not helpless despair. Sometimes, indeed, she was unable to obliterate herself, and not only stood by her guns, but carried the war into the enemy's country. I very frequently found myself between two fires, and was glad to drag what small fragments were left of me from the scene of action. In brief, the little house in Clinton Place was rapidly transforming itself into a ghastly caricature of home.

Up to the present state of affairs the colonel had never once failed to appear at dinner-time. We had become so accustomed to his ring at the prescribed hour, and to hearing him outside in the hall softly humming The Bonny Blue Flag, or I wish I was in Dixie's Land (a wish which he did not wholly monopolize)—we had, I repeat, become so accustomed to these details that one night when he absented himself we experienced a kind of alarm. It was not until the clock struck ten that we gave over expecting him. Then, fearing that possibly he was ill, I put on my hat and stepped round to Macdougal Street. Mr. Flagg had gone out late in the afternoon, and had not returned. No, he had left no word in case any one called. What had happened? I smile to myself now, and I have smiled a great many times, at the remembrance of how worried I was that night as I walked slowly back to Clinton Place.

The next evening my cousin explained his absence. He had made the acquaintance of some distinguished literary gentlemen, who had invited him to dine with them at a certain German cafe, which at an earlier date had been rather famous as the rendezvous of a group of young journalists, wits, and unblossomed poets, known as "The Bohemians." The war had caused sad havoc with these light—hearted Knights of the Long Table, and it was only upon a scattered remnant of the goodly company that the colonel had fallen. How it came about, I do not know. I know that the acquaintance presently flowered into intimacy, and that at frequent intervals after this we had a vacant chair at table. My cousin did not give himself the pains to advise us of his engagements, so these absences were not as pleasant as they would have been if we had not expected him every minute.

Recently, too, our expectation of his coming was tinged with a dread which neither I nor Mrs. Wesley had named to each other. A change was gradually taking place in my cousin. Hitherto his amiability, even when he was most unendurable, had been a part of him. Obviously he was losing that lightness of spirit which we once disliked and now began to regret. He was inclined to be excitable and sullen by turns, and often of late I had been obliged to go to the bottom of my diplomacy in preventing some painful scene. As I have said, neither my wife nor I had spoken definitely of this alteration; but the cause and nature of it could not long be ignored between us.

"How patient you are with him, dear!" said Mrs. Wesley, as I was turning out the gas after one of our grim and grotesque little dinners: the colonel had not dined with us before for a week. "I don't see how you can be so patient with the man."

"Blood is thicker than water, Clara."

"But it isn't thicker than whiskey and water, is it?"

She had said it. The colonel was drinking. It was not a question of that light elixir the precious receipt for which had been confided to him by Judge Ashburton Todhunter, of Fauquier County; it was a question of a heavier and more immediate poison. The fact that Flagg might in some desperate state drop in on us at any moment stared us in the face. That was a very serious contingency, and it was one I could not guard against. I had no false ideas touching my influence over Washington Flagg. I did not dream of attempting to influence him; I was powerless. I could do nothing but wait, and wonder what would happen. There was nothing the man might not be capable of in some insane moment.

In the meanwhile I was afraid to go out of an evening and leave Clara alone. It was impossible for us to ask a friend to dinner, though, indeed, we had not done that since my cousin dropped down on us. It was no relief that his visits grew rarer and rarer; the apprehension remained. It was no relief when they ceased altogether, for it came to that at last.

A month had elapsed since he had called at the house. I had caught sight of him once on Broadway as I was riding up town in an omnibus. He was standing at the top of the steep flight of steps that led to Herr Pfaff's saloon in the basement. It was probably Flagg's dinner hour. Mrs. Morgan, the landlady in Macdougal Street, a melancholy little soul, was now the only link between me and my kinsman. I had a weekly interview with her. I learned that Mr.

Flagg slept late, was seldom in during the day, and usually returned after midnight. A person with this eccentric scheme of life was not likely to be at home at such hours as I might find it convenient to call. Nevertheless, from time to time I knocked at the unresponsive door of his room. The two notes I had written to him he left unanswered.

All this was very grievous. He had been a trouble to me when I had him, and he was a trouble to me now I had lost him. My trouble had merely changed its color. On what downward way were his footsteps? What was to be the end of it? Sometimes I lay awake at night thinking of him. Of course, if he went to the dogs, he had nobody to blame but himself. I was not responsible for his wrong-going; nevertheless, I could not throw off my anxiety in the matter. That Flagg was leading a wild life in these days was presumable. Indeed, certain rumors to that effect were indirectly blown to me from the caves of Gambrinus. Not that I believe the bohemians demoralized him. He probably demoralized the bohemians. I began to reflect whether fate had not behaved rather handsomely, after all, in not giving me a great many relatives.

If I remember rightly, it was two months since I had laid eyes on my cousin, when, on returning home one evening, I noticed that the front door stood wide open, and had apparently been left to take care of itself. As I mounted the steps, a little annoyed at Mary's carelessness, I heard voices in the hall. Washington Flagg was standing at the foot of the staircase, with his hand on the newel-post, and Mrs. Wesley was halfway up the stairs, as if in the act of descending. I learned later that she had occupied this position for about three quarters of an hour. She was extremely pale and much agitated. Flagg's flushed face and tilted hat told his part of the story. He was not in one of his saturnine moods. He was amiably, and, if I may say it, gracefully drunk, and evidently had all his wits about him.

"I've been telling Mrs. Wesley," he began at once, as if I had been present all the while, and he was politely lifting me into the conversation—"I've been telling Mrs. Wesley that I'm a Lost Cause."

"A lost soul," was Mrs. Wesley's amendment from the staircase. "Oh, Tom, I am so glad you have come! I thought you never would! I let him in an hour or two ago, and he has kept me here ever since."

"You were so entertaining," said my cousin, with a courteous sweep of his disengaged hand, and speaking with that correctness of enunciation which sometimes survives everything.

"Flagg," I said, stepping to his side, "you will oblige me by returning to your lodgings."

"You think I'm not all right?"

"I am sure of it."

"And you don't want me here, dear old boy?"

"No, I don't want you here. The time has come for me to be frank with you, Flagg, and I see that your mind is clear enough to enable you to understand what I say."

"I reckon I can follow you, Thomas."

"My stock of romantic nonsense about kinship and family duties, and all that, has given out, and will not be renewed."

"Won't do business any more at the old stand?"

"Exactly so. I have done everything I could to help you, and you have done nothing whatever for yourself. You have not even done yourself the scant justice of treating Clara and me decently. In future you will be obliged to look after your own affairs, financial as well as social. Your best plan now is to go to work. I shall no longer concern myself with your comings and goings, except so far as to prevent you from coming here and disturbing Clara. Have you put that down?"

"Wesley, my boy, I'll pay you for this."

"If you do, it will be the first thing you have paid for since you came North."

My statement, however accurate, was not wholly delicate, and I subsequently regretted it, but when a patient man loses his patience he goes to extremes. Washington Flagg straightened himself for an instant, and then smiled upon me in an amused, patronizing way quite untranslatable.

"Thomas, that was neat, very neat—for you. When I see Judge Ashburton Todhunter I'll tell him about it. It's the sort of mild joke he likes."

"I should be proud to have Judge Ashburton Todhunter's approval of any remark of mine, but in the meanwhile it would be a greater pleasure to me to have you return at once to Macdougal Street, where, no doubt, Mrs. Morgan is delaying dinner for you."

"Say no more, Wesley. I'll never set foot in your house again, as sure as my name is Flagg—and long may I wave o'er the land of the free and the home of the brave."

"He is a kind of Flagg that I don't wish to have wave over MY home," said Mrs. Wesley, descending the stairs as my cousin with painful care closed the door softly behind him.

So the end was come. It had come with less unpleasantness than I should have predicted. The ties of kindred, too tightly stretched, had snapped; but they had snapped very gently, so to speak.

V

Washington Flagg was as good as his word, which is perhaps not a strong indorsement. He never again set foot in my house. A week afterward I found that he had quitted Macdougal Street.

"He has gone South," said Mrs. Morgan.

"Did he leave no message for me?"

"He didn't leave a message for nobody."

"Did he happen to say to what part of the South he was bound?"

"He said he was going back to Dixie's Land, and didn't say no more."

That was all. His departure had been as abrupt and unlocked for as his arrival. I wondered if he would turn up again at the end of another twenty years, and I wondered how he had paid his travelling expenses to the land of the magnolia and the persimmon. That mystery was solved a few days subsequently when a draft (for so reasonable a sum as not to be worth mentioning to Clara) was presented to me for payment at my office.

Washington Flagg was gone, but his shadow was to linger for a while longer on our household. It was difficult to realize that the weight which had oppressed us had been removed. We were scarcely conscious of how heavy it had been until it was lifted. I was now and then forced to make an effort not to expect the colonel to dinner.

A month or two after his disappearance an incident occurred which brought him back very vividly and in a somewhat sinister shape to our imaginations. Quite late one night there was a sharp ring at the door. Mary having gone to bed, I answered the bell. On the doorstep stood a tall, pale girl, rather shabbily dressed, but with a kind of beauty about her; it seemed to flash from her eyelashes, which I noticed were very heavy. The hall light fell full upon this slight figure, standing there wrapped in an insufficient shawl, against a dense background of whirling snowflakes. She asked if I could give her Colonel Flagg's address. On receiving my reply, the girl swiftly descended the steps, and vanished into the darkness. There was a tantalizing point of romance and mystery to all this. As I slowly closed the front door I felt that perhaps I was closing it on a tragedy—one of those piteous, unwritten tragedies of the great city. I have wondered a thousand times who that girl was and what became of her.

Before the end of the year another incident—this time with a touch of comedy—lighted up the past of my kinsman. Among the travelling agents for the Savonarola Fire Insurance Company was a young man by the name of Brett, Charles Brett, a new employee. His family had been ruined by the war, and he had wandered North, as the son of many a Southern gentleman had been obliged to do, to earn his living. We became friends, and frequently lunched together when his business brought him to the city. Brett had been in the Confederate army, and it occurred to me one day to ask him if he had ever known my cousin the colonel. Brett was acquainted with a George W. Flagg; had known him somewhat intimately, in fact; but it was probably not the same man. We compared notes, and my Flagg was his Flagg.

"But he wasn't a colonel," said Brett. "Why, Flagg wasn't in the war at all. I don't fancy he heard a gun fired, unless it went off by accident in some training-camp for recruits. He got himself exempt from service in the field by working in the government saltworks. A heap of the boys escaped conscription that way."

In the saltworks! That connected my cousin with the navy rather than with the army!

I would have liked not to believe Brett's statement, but it was so circumstantial and precise as not to be doubted. Brett was far from suspecting how deeply his information had cut me. In spite of my loyalty, the discovery that my kinsman had not been a full-blown rebel was vastly humiliating. How that once curiously regarded flower of chivalry had withered! What about those reckless moonlight raids? What had become of Prince Rupert, at the head of his plumed cavaliers, sweeping through the valley of the Shenandoah, and dealing merited destruction to the boys in blue? In view of Brett's startling revelation, my kinsman's personal anecdotes of Stonewall Jackson took on an amusing quality which they had not possessed for us in the original telling.

I was disappointed that Clara's astonishment was much more moderate than mine.

"He was TOO brave, Tom, dear. He always seemed to be overdoing it just a grain, don't you think?"

I didn't think so at the time; I was afraid he was telling the truth. And now, by one of those contradictions inseparable from weak humanity, I regretted that he was not. A hero had tumbled from the family pedestal—a misguided hero, to be sure, but still a hero. My vanity, which in this case was of a complex kind, had received a shock.

I did not recover from it for nearly three months, when I received a second shock of a more serious nature. It came in the shape of a letter, dated at Pensacola, Florida, and written by one Sylvester K. Matthews, advising me that George Flagg had died of the yellow fever in that city the previous month. I gathered from the letter that the writer had been with my cousin through his illness, and was probably an intimate friend; at all events the details of the funeral had fallen to the charge of Mr. Matthews, who enclosed the receipted bills with the remark that he had paid them, but supposed that I would prefer to do so, leaving it, in a way, at my option.

The news of my cousin's death grieved me more than I should have imagined beforehand. He had not appreciated my kindness; he had not added to my happiness while I was endeavoring to secure his; he had been flagrantly ungrateful, and in one or two minor matters had deceived me. Yet, after all said and done, he was my cousin, my only cousin—and he was dead. Let us criticise the living, but spare the dead.

I put the memoranda back into the envelope; they consisted of a bill for medical attendance, a board bill, the nurse's account, and an undertaker's bill, with its pathetic and, to me, happily, unfamiliar items. For the rest of the day I was unable to fix my attention on my work, or to compose myself sufficiently to write to Mr. Matthews. I quitted the office that evening an hour earlier than was my habit.

Whether Clara was deeply affected by what had happened, or whether she disapproved of my taking upon myself expenses which, under the peculiar circumstances, might properly be borne by Flagg's intimate friend and comrade, was something I could not determine. She made no comments. If she considered that I had already done all that my duty demanded of me to do for my cousin, she was wise enough not to say so; for she must have seen that I took a different and unalterable view of it. Clara has her own way fifty-nine minutes out of the hour, but the sixtieth minute is mine.

She was plainly not disposed to talk on the subject; but I wanted to talk with some one on the subject; so, when dinner was through, I put the Matthews papers into my pocket and went up to my friend Bleeker's, in Seventeenth Street. Though a little cynical at times, he was a man whose judgment I thought well of.

After reading the letter and glancing over the memoranda, Bleeker turned to me and said, "You want to know how it strikes me—is that it?"

"Well—yes."

"The man is dead?"

"Yes."

"And buried?"

"Assuredly."

"And the bills are paid?"

"You see yourself they are receipted."

"Well, then," said Bleeker, "considering all things, I should let well enough alone."

"You mean you would do nothing in the matter?"

"I should 'let the dead past bury its dead,' as Longfellow says." Bleeker was always quoting Longfellow.

"But it isn't the dead past, it's the living present that has attended to the business; and he has sent in his account with all the items. I can't have this Matthews going about the country telling everybody that I allowed him to pay my cousin's funeral expenses."

"Then pay them. You have come to me for advice after making up your mind to follow your own course. That's just the way people do when they really want to be advised. I've done it myself, Wesley—I've done it myself."

The result was, I sent Mr. Matthews a check, after which I impulsively threw those dreadful bills into the office grate. I had no right to do it, for the vouchers really belonged to Mr. Matthews, and might be wanted some day; but they had haunted me like so many ghosts until I destroyed them. I fell asleep that night trying to recollect whether the items included a head-stone for my cousin's grave. I couldn't for the life of me remember, and it troubled me not a little. There were enough nameless graves in the South, without his being added to the number.

One day, a fortnight later, as Clara and I were finishing dinner, young Brett called at the house. I had supposed him to be in Omaha. He had, in effect, just come from there and elsewhere on one of his long business tours, and had arrived in the city too late in the afternoon to report himself at the office. He now dropped in merely for a moment, but we persuaded him to remain and share the dessert with us. I purposed to keep him until Clara left us to our cigars. I wished to tell him of my cousin's death, which I did not care to do, while she was at the table. We were talking of this and that, when Brett looked up, and said rather abruptly—

"By the way, I saw Flagg on the street the other day in Mobile. He was looking well."

The bit of melon I had in my mouth refused to be swallowed. I fancy that my face was a study. A dead silence followed; and then my wife reached across the table, and pressing my hand, said very gently—

"Wesley, you were not brilliant, but you were good."

All this was longer ago than I care to remember. I heard no more from Mr. Matthews. Last week, oddly enough, while glancing over a file of recent Southern newspapers, I came upon the announcement of the death of George W. Flagg. It was yellow fever this time also. If later on I receive any bills in connection with that event, I shall let my friend Bleeker audit them.

"FOR BRAVERY ON THE FIELD OF BATTLE"

I

The recruiting-office at Rivermouth was in a small, unpainted, weather-stained building on Anchor Street, not far from the custom-house. The tumble-down shell had long remained tenantless, and now, with its mouse-colored exterior, easily lent itself to its present requirements as a little military mouse-trap. In former years it had been occupied as a thread-and-needle and candy shop by one Dame Trippew. All such petty shops in the town were always kept by old women, and these old women were always styled dames. It is to be lamented that they and their innocent traffic have vanished into the unknown.

The interior of the building, consisting of one room and an attic covered by a lean-to roof, had undergone no change beyond the removal of Dame Trippew's pathetic stock at the time of her bankruptcy. The narrow counter, painted pea-green and divided in the centre by a swinging gate, still stretched from wall to wall at the farther end of the room, and behind the counter rose a series of small wooden drawers, which now held nothing but a fleeting and inaccurate memory of the lavender, and pennyroyal, and the other sweet herbs that used to be deposited in them. Even the tiny cow-bell, which once served to warn Dame Trippew of the advent of a customer, still hung from a bit of curved iron on the inner side of the street-door, and continued to give out a petulant, spasmodic jingle whenever that door was opened, however cautiously. If the good soul could have returned to the scene of her terrestrial commerce, she might have resumed business at the old stand without making any alterations whatever. Everything remained precisely as she had left it at the instant of her exit. But a wide gulf separated Dame Trippew from the present occupant of the premises. Dame Trippew's slight figure, with its crisp, snowy cap and apron, and steel-bowed spectacles, had been replaced by the stalwart personage of a sergeant of artillery in the regular army, between whose overhanging red mustache and the faint white down that had of late years come to Dame Trippew's upper lip, it would have been impossible to establish a parallel. The only things these two might have claimed in common were a slackness of trade and a liking for the aromatic Virginia leaf, though Dame Trippew had taken hers in a dainty idealistic powder, and the sergeant took his in realistic plug through the medium of an aggressive clay pipe.

In spite of the starry shield, supported by two crossed cannon cut out of tin and surmounted by the national bird in the same material, which hung proudly over the transom outside; in spite of the drummer-boy from the fort, who broke the silence into slivers at intervals throughout the day; in brief, in spite of his own martial bearing and smart uniform, the sergeant found trade very slack. At Rivermouth the war with Mexico was not a popular undertaking. If there were any heroic blood left in the old town by the sea, it appeared to be in no hurry to come forward and get itself shed. There were hours in which Sergeant O'Neil despaired of his country. But by degrees the situation brightened, recruits began to come in, and finally the town and the outlying districts—chiefly the outlying districts—managed to furnish a company for the State regiment. One or two prominent citizens had been lured by commissions as officers; but neither of the two Rivermouthians who went in as privates was of the slightest civic importance. One of these men was named James Dutton.

Why on earth James Dutton wanted to go to the war was a puzzle to the few townsfolk who had any intimate acquaintance with the young man. Intimate acquaintance is perhaps too strong a term; for though Button was born in the town and had always lived there, he was more or less a stranger to those who knew him best. Comrades he had, of course, in a manner: the boys with whom he had formerly gone to the public school, and two or three maturer persons whose acquaintance he had contracted later in the way of trade. But with these he could scarcely be said to be intimate. James Dutton's rather isolated condition was not in consequence of any morbid or uncouth streak in his mental make-up. He was of a shy and gentle nature, and his sedentary occupation had simply let the habit of solitude and unsociability form a shell about him. Dutton was a shoemaker and cobbler, like his father before him, plying his craft in the shabby cottage where he was born and had lived ever since, at the foot of a narrow lane leading down to the river—a lonely, doleful sort of place, enlivened with a bit of shelving sand where an ancient fisherman occasionally came to boil lobsters.

In the open lots facing the unhinged gate was an old relinquished tannery that still flavored the air with decayed hemlock and fir bark, which lay here and there in dull-red patches, killing the grass. The undulations of a colonial graveyard broke tamely against the western base of the house. Head-stones and monuments—if there had ever been any monuments—had melted away. Only tradition and those slowly subsiding wave-like ridges of graves revealed the character of the spot. Within the memory of man nobody had been dropped into that Dead Sea. The Duttons, father and son, had dwelt here nearly twenty-four years. They owned the shanty. The old man was now dead, having laid down his awl and lapstone just a year before the rise of those international complications which resulted in the appearance of Sergeant O'Neil in Rivermouth, where he immediately tacked up the blazoned aegis of the United States over the doorway of Dame Trippew's little shop.

As has been indicated, the war with Mexico was not looked upon with favor by the inhabitants of Rivermouth, who clearly perceived its underlying motive—the extension of slave territory. The abolition element in the town had instantly been blown to a white heat. Moreover, war in itself, excepting as a defensive measure or on a point of honor, seemed rather poor business to the thrifty Rivermouthians. They were wholly of the opinion of Birdofredom Sawin, that

"Nimepunce a day fer killin' folks comes kind o' low fer murder."

That old Nehemiah Dutton's son should have any interest one way or the other in the questions involved was inconceivable, and the morning he presented himself at the recruiting-office a strong ripple of surprise ran over the group of idlers that hung day after day around the door of the crazy tenement, drawn thither by the drum-taps and a morbid sense of gunpowder in the air. These idlers were too sharp or too unpatriotic to enlist themselves, but they had unbounded enthusiasm for those who did. After a moment's hesitation, they cheered Jemmy Dutton handsomely.

On the afternoon of his enlistment, he was met near the post-office by Marcellus Palfrey, the sexton of the Old Brick Church.

"What are you up to, anyhow, Jemmy?" asked Palfrey. "What's your idee?"

"My idea is," replied Dutton, "that I've never been able to live freely and respectably, as I've wanted to live; but I mean to die like a gentleman, when it comes to that."

"What do you call a gentleman, Jemmy?"

"Well, a man who serves faithfully, and stands by to lay down his life for his duty—he's a gentleman."

"That's so," said Palfrey. "He needn't have no silver-plated handles, nor much outside finish, if he's got a satin linin'. He's one of God's men."

What really sent James Dutton to the war? Had he some unformulated and hitherto unsuspected dream of military glory, or did he have an eye to supposable gold ingots piled up in the sub-basement of the halls of the Montezumas? Was it a case of despised love, or was he simply tired of re-heeling and re-soling the boots of Rivermouth folk; tired to death of the river that twice a day crept up to lap the strip of sandy beach at the foot of Nutter's Lane; tired to death of being alone, and poor, and aimless? His motive is not positively to be known, only to be guessed at. We shall not trouble ourselves about it. Neither shall the war, which for a moment casts a lurid light on his figure, delay us long. It was a tidy, comfortable little war, not without picturesque aspects. Out of its flame and smoke leaped two or three fine names that dazzled men's eyes awhile; and among the fortunate was a silent young lieutenant of infantry—a taciturn, but not unamiable young lieutenant—who was afterward destined to give the name of a great general into the keeping of history forever. Wrapped up somewhere in this Mexican war is the material for a brief American epic; but it is not to be unrolled and recited here.

II

With the departure of Our Country's Gallant Defenders, as they were loosely denominated by some—the Idiots, as they were compactly described by others—monotony again settled down upon Rivermouth. Sergeant O'Neil's heraldic emblems disappeared from Anchor Street, and the quick rattle of the tenor drum at five o'clock in the morning no longer disturbed the repose of peace-loving citizens. The tide of battle rolled afar, and its echoes were not of a quality to startle the drowsy old seaport. Indeed, it had little at stake. Only four men had gone from the town proper. One, Captain Kittery, died before reaching the seat of war; one deserted on the way; one, Lieutenant Bangs, was sent home invalided; and only James Dutton was left to represent the land force of his native town. He might as well have died or deserted, for he was promptly forgotten.

From time to time accounts of battles and bombardments were given in the columns of the Rivermouth Barnacle, on which occasions the Stars and Stripes, held in the claws of a spread eagle, decorated the editorial page—a cut which until then had been used only to celebrate the bloodless victories of the ballot. The lists of dead, wounded, and missing were always read with interest or anxiety, as might happen, for one had friends and country acquaintances, if not fellow-townsmen, with the army on the Rio Grande. Meanwhile nobody took the trouble to bestow a thought on James Dutton. He was as remote and shadowy in men's memories as if he had been killed at Thermopylae or Bunker's Hill. But one day the name of James Dutton blazed forth in a despatch that electrified the community. At the storming of Chapultepec, Private James Dutton, Company K, Rivermouth, had done a very valorous deed. He had crawled back to a plateau on the heights, from which the American troops had been driven, and had brought off his captain, who had been momentarily stunned by the wind of a round-shot. Not content with that, Private Dutton had returned to the dangerous plateau, and, under a heavy fire, had secured a small field-piece which was about to fall into the hands of the enemy. Later in the day this little howitzer did eminent service. After touching on one or two other minor matters, the despatch remarked, incidentally, that Private James Dutton had had his left leg blown off.

The name of James Dutton was instantly on every lip in town. Citizens who had previously ignored his existence, or really had not been aware of it, were proud of him. The Hon. Jedd Deane said that he had. long regarded James Dutton as a young man of great promise, a—er—most remarkable young person, in short; one of the kind with much—er—latent ability. Postmaster Mugridge observed, with the strong approval of those who heard him, that young Dutton was nobody's fool, though what especial wisdom Dutton had evinced in having his leg blown off was not clear. Captain Tewksberry, commanding the local militia company, the Rivermouth Tigers, was convinced that no one who had not carefully studied Scott's Tactics could have brought away that gun under the circumstances. "Here, you will observe, was the exposed flank of the heights; there, behind the chevaux-de-frise, lay the enemy," etc., etc. Dutton's former school-fellows began to remember that there had always been something tough and gritty in Jim Dutton. The event was one not to be passed over by Parson Wibird Hawkins, who made a most direct reference to it in his Sunday's sermon—Job xxxix. 25: "He saith among the trumpets, Ha, ha; and he smelleth the battle afar off, the thunder of the captains, and the shouting."

After the first burst of local pride and enthusiasm had exhausted itself over young Dutton's brilliant action, the grim fact connected with young Dutton's left leg began to occupy the public mind. The despatch had vaguely hinted at amputation, and had stopped there. If his leg had been shot away, was it necessary that the rest of him should be amputated? In the opinion of Schoolmaster Grimshaw, such treatment seemed almost tautological. However, all was presumably over by this time. Had poor Dutton died under the operation? Solicitude on that point was widespread and genuine. Later official intelligence relieved the stress of anxiety. Private Dutton had undergone the operation successfully and with great fortitude; he was doing well, and as soon as it was possible for him to bear transportation he was to be sent home. He had been complimented in the commanding officer's report of the action to headquarters, and General Winfield Scott had sent Private Dutton a silver medal "for bravery on the field of battle." If the Government had wanted one or two hundred volunteers from Rivermouth, that week was the week to get them.

Then intervened a long silence touching James Dutton. This meant feverish nights and weary days in hospital, and finally blissful convalescence, when the scent of the orange and magnolia blossoms blown in at the open window seemed to James Dutton a richer recompense than he deserved for his martyrdom. At last he was in condition to be put on board a transport for New Orleans. Thence a man-of-war was to convey him to Rivermouth, where the ship was to be overhauled and have its own wounds doctored.

When it was announced from the fort that the vessel bearing James Dutton had been sighted off the coast and would soon be in the Narrows, the town was thrown into such a glow of excitement as it had not experienced since the day a breathless and bedraggled man on horseback had dashed into Rivermouth with the news that the Sons of Liberty in Boston had pitched the British tea overboard. The hero of Chapultepec—the only hero Rivermouth had had since the colonial period—was coming up the Narrows! It is odd that three fourths of anything should be more estimable than the whole, supposing the whole to be estimable. When James Dutton had all his limbs he was lightly esteemed, and here was Rivermouth about to celebrate a fragment of him.

The normally quiet and unfrequented street leading down to the boat-landing was presently thronged by Rivermouthians—men, women, and children. The arrival of a United States vessel always stirred an emotion in the town. Naval officers were prime favorites in aristocratic circles, and there were few ships in the service that did not count among their blue-jackets one or more men belonging to the port. Thus all sea-worn mariners in Uncle Sam's employ were sure of both patrician and democratic welcome at Rivermouth. But the present ship contained an especially valuable cargo.

It was a patient and characteristically undemonstrative crowd that assembled on the wharf, a crowd content to wait an hour or more without a murmur after the ship had dropped anchor in midstream for the captain's gig to be lowered from the davits. The shrill falsetto of the boatswain's whistle suddenly informed those on shore of what was taking place on the starboard side, and in a few minutes the gig came sweeping across the blue water, with James Dutton seated in the stern-sheets and looking very pale. He sat there, from time to time pulling his blond mustache, evidently embarrassed. A cheer or two rose from the wharf when the eight gleaming blades simultaneously stood upright in air, as if the movement had been performed by some mechanism. The disembarkment followed in dead silence, for the interest was too novel and too intense to express itself noisily. Those nearest to James Dutton pressed forward to shake hands with him, but this ceremony had to be dispensed with as he hobbled on his crutches through the crowd, piloted by Postmaster Mugridge to the hack which stood in waiting at the head of the wharf.

Dutton was driven directly to his own little cottage in Nutter's Lane, which had been put in order for his occupancy. The small grocery closet had been filled with supplies, the fire had been lighted in the diminutive kitchen stove, and the tea-kettle was twittering on top, like a bird on a bough. The Twombly girls, Priscilla and Mehitabel, had set some pansies and lilacs here and there in blue china mugs, and decorated with greenery the faded daguerreotype of old Nehemiah Dutton, which hung like a slowly dissolving ghost over his ancient shoemaker's bench. As James Dutton hobbled into the contracted room where he had spent the tedious years of his youth and manhood, he had to lift a hand from one of the crutches to brush away the tears that blinded him. It was so good to be at home again!

[Illustration with caption: Held an informal reception]

That afternoon, Dutton held an informal reception. There was a constant coming and going of persons not in the habit of paying visits in so unfashionable a neighborhood as Nutter's Lane. Now and then a townsman, conscious that his unimportance did not warrant his unintroduced presence inside, lounged carelessly by the door; and through the rest of the day several small boys turned somersaults and skylarked under the window, or sat in rows on the rail fence opposite the gate. Among others came the Hon. Jedd Deane, with his most pronounced Websterian air—he was always oscillating between the manner of Webster and that of Rufus Choate—to pay his respects to James Dutton, which was considered a great compliment indeed. A few days later, this statesman invited Dutton to dine with him at the ancestral mansion in Mulberry Avenue, in company with Parson Wibird Hawkins, Postmaster Mugridge, and Silas Trefethen, the Collector of the Port. It was intimated that young Dutton had handled himself under this ordeal with as much self-possession and dignity as if he had always dined off colonial china, and had always stirred his after-dinner coffee with a spoon manufactured by Paul Revere.

A motion to give James Dutton a limited public banquet, at which the politicians could have a chance to unfold their eloquence, was discussed and approved by the Board of Selectmen, but subsequently laid on the table, it being reported that Mr. Dutton had declared that he would rather have his other leg blown off than make a speech. This necessarily killed the project, for a reply from him to the chairman's opening address was a sine qua non.

Life now opened up all sunshine to James Dutton. His personal surroundings were of the humblest, but it was home, sweet, sweet home. One may roam amid palaces—even amid the halls of the Montezumas—yet, after all, one's own imperfect drain is the best. The very leather-parings and bits of thread that had drifted from the work-bench into the front yard, and seemed to have taken root there like some strange exotic weed, were a delight to him. Dutton's inability to move about as in former years sometimes irked him, but everything else was pleasant. He resolved to make the best of this one misfortune, since without it he would never have been treated with such kindness and consideration. The constant employment he found at his trade helped him to forget that he had not two legs. A man who is obliged to occupy a cobbler's bench day after day has no special need of legs at all. Everybody brought jobs to his door, and Dutton had as much work as he could do. At times, indeed, he was forced to decline a commission. He could hardly credit his senses when this occurred.

So life ran very smoothly with him. For the first time in his existence he found himself humming or whistling an accompaniment to the rat-tat-tat of his hammer on the sole-leather. No hour of the twenty-four hung heavily on him. In the rear of the cottage was a bit of ground, perhaps forty feet square, with an old elm in the centre, under which Dutton liked to take his nooning. It was here he used to play years ago, a quiet, dreamy lad, with no companions except the squirrels. A family of them still inhabited the ancient boughs, and it amused him to remember how he once believed that the nimble brown creatures belonged to a tribe of dwarf Indians who might attempt to scalp him with their little knives if they caught him out after dusk. Though his childhood had not been happy, he had reached a bend in the road where to pause and look back was to find the retrospect full of fairy lights and coloring.

Almost every evening one or two old acquaintances, with whom he had not been acquainted, dropped in to chat with him, mainly about the war. He had shared in all the skirmishes and battles from Cerro Gordo and Molino del Rey up to the capture of Chapultepec; and it was something to hear of these matters from one who had been a part of what he saw. It was considered a favor to be allowed to examine at short range that medal "for bravery on the field of battle." It was a kind of honor "just to heft it," as somebody said one night. There were visitors upon whom the impression was strong that General Scott had made the medal with his own hands.

James Dutton was ever modest in speaking of his single personal exploit. He guessed he didn't know what he was doing at the moment when he tumbled the howitzer into the ravine, from which the boys afterward fished it out. "You see, things were anyway up on that plateau. The copper bullets were flying like hailstones, so it didn't much matter where a fellow went—he was sure to get peppered. Of course the captain couldn't be left up there—we wanted him for morning parades. Then I happened to see the little field-piece stranded among the chaparral. It was a cursed nice little cannon. It would have been a blighting shame to have lost it."

"I suppose you didn't leave your heart down there along with the senoriteers, did you, Jemmy?" inquired a town Lovelace.

"No," said Dutton, always perfectly matter of fact; "I left my leg."

Ah, yes; life was very pleasant to him in those days!

Not only kindnesses, but honors were showered upon him. Parson Wibird Hawkins, in the course of an address before the Rivermouth Historical and Genealogical Society, that winter, paid an eloquent tribute to "the glorious military career of our young townsman"—which was no more than justice; for if a man who has had a limb shot off in battle has not had a touch of glory, then war is an imposition. Whenever a distinguished stranger visited the town, he was not let off without the question, "Are you aware, sir, that we have among us one of the heroes of the late Mexican war?" And then a stroll about town to the various points of historic interest invariably ended at the unpretending doorstep of Dutton's cottage.

At the celebration of the first Fourth of July following his return from Mexico, James Dutton was pretty nearly, if not quite, the chief feature of the procession, riding in an open barouche immediately behind that of the Governor. The boys would have marched him all by himself if it had been possible to form him into a hollow square. From this day James Dutton, in his faded coat and battered artillery cap, was held an indispensable adjunct to all turnouts of a warlike complexion. Nor was his fame wholly local. Now and then, as time went on, some old comrade of the Army of the Rio Grande, a member perhaps of old Company K, would turn up in Rivermouth for no other apparent purpose than to smoke a pipe or so with Button at his headquarters in Nutter's Lane. If he sometimes chanced to furnish the caller with a dollar or two of "the sinews of war," it was nobody's business. The days on which these visits fell were red-letter days to James Dutton.

It was a proud moment when he found himself one afternoon sitting, at Schoolmaster Grimshaw's invitation, on the platform in the recitation-room of the Temple Grammar School—sitting on the very platform with the green baize-covered table to which he had many a time marched up sideways to take a feruling. Something of the old awe and apprehension which Master Grimshaw used to inspire crept over him. There were instants when Dutton would have abjectly held out his hand if he had been told to do it. He had been invited to witness the evolutions of the graduating class in history and oratory, and the moisture gathered in his honest blue eyes when a panic-stricken urchin faltered forth—

"We were not many, we who stood before the iron sleet that day."

Dutton listened to it all with unruffled gravity. There was never a more gentle hero, or one with a slighter sense of humor, than the hero of Chapultepec.

Dutton's lot was now so prosperous as to exclude any disturbing thoughts concerning the future. The idea of applying for a pension never entered his head until the subject was suggested to him by Postmaster Mugridge, a more worldly man, an office-holder himself, with a carefully peeled eye on Government patronage. Dutton then reflected that perhaps a pension would be handy in his old age, when he could not expect to work steadily at his trade, even if he were able to work at all. He looked about him for somebody to manage the affair for him. Lawyer Penhallow undertook the business with alacrity; but the alacrity was all on his side, for there were thousands of yards of red tape to be unrolled at Washington before anything in that sort could be done. At that conservative stage of our national progress, it was not possible for a man to obtain a pension simply because he happened to know the brother of a man who knew another man that had intended to go to the war, and didn't. Dutton's claims, too, were seriously complicated by the fact that he had lost his discharge papers; so the matter dragged, and was still dragging when it ceased to be of any importance to anybody.

Whenever James Dutton glanced into the future, it was with a tranquil mind. He pictured himself, should he not fall out of the ranks, a white-haired, possibly a bald-headed old boy, sitting of summer evenings on the doorstep of his shop, and telling stories to the children—the children and grandchildren of his present associates and friends. He would naturally have laid up something by that time; besides, there was his pension. Meanwhile, though he moved in a humble sphere, was not his lot an enviable one? There were long years of pleasant existence to be passed through before he reached the period of old age. Of course that would have its ailments and discomforts, but its compensations, also. It seemed scarcely predictable that the years to come held for him either great sorrows or great felicities: he would never marry, and though he might have to grieve over a fallen comrade here and there, his heart was not to be wrung by the possible death of wife or child. With the tints of the present he painted his simple future, and was content.

Sometimes the experiences of the last few years took on the semblance of a haunting dream; those long marches through a land rich with strange foliage and fruits, the enchanted Southern nights, the life in camp, the roar of battle, and that one bewildering day on the heights of Chapultepec—it all seemed phantasmagoric. But there was his mutilation to assure him of the reality, and there on Anchor Street, growing grayer and more wrinkled every season, stood the little building where he had enlisted. To be sure, the shield was gone from the transom, and the spiders had stretched their reticulated barricades across the entrance; but whenever Dutton hobbled by the place, he could almost see Sergeant O'Neil leaning in an insidious attitude against the door-sill, and smoking his short clay pipe as of old. Yet as time elapsed, this figure also grew indistinct and elusive, like the rest. Possibly—but this is the merest conjecture, and has bearing only on a later period—possibly it may have sometimes occurred to James Dutton, in a vague way, that after all there had been something ironical and sinister in his good fortune. The very circumstance that had lifted him from his obscurity had shut him out from further usefulness in life; his one success had defeated him; he was stranded, and could do no more. If such a reflection ever came to him, no expression of it found a way to his lips.

The weeks turned themselves into months, and the months into years. Perhaps four years had passed by when clouds of a perceptible density began to gather on James Dutton's bright horizon.

The wisest of poets has told us that custom dulls the edge of appetite. One gets used to everything, even to heroes. James Dutton was beginning to lose the bloom of his novelty. Indeed, he had already lost it. The process had been so gradual, so subtle, in its working, that the final result came upon him like something that had happened suddenly. But this was not the fact. He might have seen it coming, if he had watched. One by one his customers had drifted away from him; his shop was out of the beaten track, and a fashionable boot and shoe establishment, newly sprung up in the business part of the town, had quietly absorbed his patrons. There was no conscious unkindness in this desertion. Thoughtless neglect, all the more bitter by contrast, had followed thoughtless admiration. Admiration and neglect are apt to hunt in couples. Nearly all the customers left on Dutton's hands had resolved themselves into two collateral classes, those who delayed and those who forgot to pay. That unreached pension, which flitted like an ignis fatuus the instant one got anywhere near it, would have been very handy to have just then. The want of it had come long before old age. Dutton was only twenty-nine. Yet he somehow seemed old. The indoor confinement explained his pallor, but not the deepening lines that recently began to spread themselves fan-like at the corners of his eyes.

Callers at Nutter's Lane had now become rare birds. The dwindling of his visitors had at first scarcely attracted his notice; it had been so gradual, like the rest. But at last Dutton found himself alone. The old solitude of his youth had re-knitted its shell around him. Now that he was unsustained by the likelihood of some one looking in on him, the evenings, especially the winter evenings, were long to Dutton. Owing to weak eyes, he was unable to read much, and then he was not naturally a reader. He was too proud or too shy to seek the companionship which he might have found at Meeks's drug-store. Moreover, the society there was not of a kind that pleased him; it had not pleased him in the old days, and now he saw how narrow and poor it was, having had a glimpse of the broad world. The moonlight nights, when he could sit at the window, and look out on the gleaming river and the objects on the farther shore, were bearable. Something seemed always to be going on in the old disused burying-ground; he was positive that on certain nights uncanny figures flitted from dark to dark through a broad intervening belt of silvery moonshine. A busy spot after all these years! But when it was pitch-black outside, he had no resources. His work-bench with its polished concave leather seat, the scanty furniture, and his father's picture on the wall, grew hateful to him. At an hour when the social life of the town was at its beginning, he would extinguish his melancholy tallow-dip and go to bed, lying awake until long after all the rest of the world slumbered. This lying awake soon became a habit. The slightest sound broke his sleep—the gnawing of a mouse behind the mopboard, or a change in the wind; and then insomnia seized upon him. He lay there listening to the summer breeze among the elms, or to the autumn winds that, sweeping up from the sea, teased his ear with muffled accents of wrecked and drowning men.

The pay for the few jobs which came to him at this juncture was insufficient to supply many of his simple wants. It was sometimes a choice with him between food and fuel. When he was younger, he used to get all the chips and kindling he wanted from Sherburn's shipyard, three quarters of a mile away. But handicapped as he now was, it was impossible for him to compass that distance over the slippery sidewalk or through the drifted road-bed. During the particular winter here in question, James Dutton was often cold, and oftener hungry—and nobody suspected it.

A word in the ear of Parson Wibird Hawkins, or the Hon. Jedd Deane, or any of the scores of kind-hearted townsfolk, would have changed the situation. But to make known his distress, to appeal for charity, to hold out his hand and be a pauper—that was not in him. From his point of view, if he could have done that, he would not have been the man to rescue his captain on the fiery plateau, and then go back through that hell of musketry to get the mountain howitzer. He was secretly and justly proud of saving his captain's life and of bringing off that "cursed nice little cannon." He gloried over it many a time to himself, and often of late took the medal of honor from its imitation-morocco case, and read the inscription by the light of his flickering candle. The embossed silver words seemed to spread a lambent glow over all the squalid little cabin—seemed almost to set it on fire! More than once some irrepressible small boy, prowling at night in the neighborhood and drawn like a moth by the flame of Dutton's candle, had set his eye to a crack in the door-panel and seen the shoemaker sitting on the edge of his bed with the medal in his hand.

Until within a year or eighteen months, Dutton had regularly attended the Sunday morning service at the Old Brick Church. One service was all he could manage, for it was difficult for him to mount the steep staircase leading to his seat in the gallery. That his attendance slackened and finally ceased altogether, he tried, in his own mind, to attribute to this difficulty, and not to the fact that his best suit had become so threadbare as to make him ashamed; though the congregation now seldom glanced up, as it used to do, at the organ-loft where he sat separated from the choir by a low green curtain. Thus he had on his hands the whole unemployed day, with no break in its monotony; and it often seemed interminable. The Puritan Sabbath as it then existed was not a thing to be trifled with. All temporal affairs were sternly set aside; earth came to a standstill. Dutton, however, conceived the plan of writing down in a little blank-book the events of his life. The task would occupy and divert him, and be no flagrant sin. But there had been no events in his life until the one great event; so his autobiography resolved itself into a single line on the first page—

Sept. 13, 1847. Had my leg shot off.

What else was there to record, except a transient gleam of sunshine immediately after his return home, and his present helplessness and isolation?

It was one morning at the close of a particularly bitter December. The river-shore was sheathed in thicker ice than had been known for twenty years. The cold snap, with its freaks among water-pipes and window-glass and straw-bedded roots in front gardens, was a thing that was to be remembered and commented on for twenty years to come. All natural phenomena have a curious attraction for persons who live in small towns and villages. The weathercock on the spire and the barometer on the back piazza are studied as they are not studied by dwellers in cities. A habit of keen observation of trivial matters becomes second nature in rural places. The provincial eye grows as sharp as the woodsman's. Thus it happened that somebody passing casually through Nutter's Lane that morning noticed—noticed it as a thing of course, since it was so—that no smoke was coming out of Dutton's chimney. The observer presently mentioned the fact at the Brick Market up town, and some of the bystanders began wondering if Dutton had overslept himself, or if he were under the weather. Nobody recollected seeing him lately, and nobody recollected not seeing him; a person so seldom in the street as Dutton is not soon missed. Dr. Meeks concluded that he would look in at Nutter's Lane on the way home with his marketing. The man who had remarked the absence of smoke had now a blurred impression that the shutters of Dutton's shop-window had not been taken down. It looked as if things were not quite right with him. Two or three persons were going in Dr. Meeks's direction, so they accompanied him, and turned into Nutter's Lane with the doctor.

The shop-shutters were still up, and no feather of smoke was curling from the one chimney of Dutton's little house. Dr. Meeks rapped smartly on the door without bringing a response. After waiting a moment he knocked again, somewhat more heavily, but with like ill success. Then he tried the latch. The door was bolted.

"I think the lad must be sick," said Dr. Meeks, glancing hurriedly over his shoulder at his companions. "What shall we do?"

"I guess we'd better see if he is," said a man named Philbrick. "Let me come there," and without further words Philbrick pressed his full weight against the pine-wood panels. The rusty fastening gave way, and the door flew open. Cold as it was without, a colder breath seemed to issue from the interior. The door opened directly into the main apartment, which was Dutton's shop and sleeping-place in one. It was a lovely morning, and the sunshine, as if it had caught a glitter from the floating points of ice on the river, poured in through a rear window and flooded the room with gold. James Dutton was lying on his pallet in the farther corner. He was dead. He must have been dead several hours, perhaps two or three days. The medal lay on his breast, from which his right hand had evidently slipped. The down-like frost on the medal was so thick as to make it impossible to distinguish the words—

"FOR BRAVERY ON THE FIELD OF BATTLE."

Milton Keynes UK
Ingram Content Group UK Ltd.
UKHW021941160724
445389UK00010B/449